When Fate Turns a Corner

TO Angela, a trip home to Los Angeles to see her mother seemed like a great way to break from the old and embrace the new. But the complications of the past just won't stay in the past.

As her train nears its destination, things begin to happen that are a far cry from anything Angela ever expected. A simple little visit turns upside-down with profound effects on Angela's life and the lives of many others.

A mysterious note ultimately leads to a startling shift in family dynamics. A questionable death brings revelations of past indiscretions and present-day consequences. A psychic of unknown repute drops hints with incredible repercussions.

Old questions are answered but new ones are asked as Angela and her growing family navigate the treacherous twists and turns of fate. Angela's strength of character and her new confidence as an independent woman are put to the test.

Haze and smog often hang over the city. But especially after a storm, the day is clear and you can, indeed, see LA.

ABRENDAL AUSTIN is an award winning author who has had as broad a range of experience as the characters she writes about. Born in Valdosta, Georgia and raised in Norwalk, Connecticut, she has raised 4 children of her own and now has 8 grandchildren. Abrendal's  first book, *A Fugitive's Wife*, received wide acclaim and has launched a series of Angela Jones novels. Abrendal currently lives in Los Angeles, California. But she likes to move around so there's no telling where she will turn up next.

On a Clear Day
You Can See L.A.

© 2008 by Abrendal Austin
Black Penny Press
5198 Arlington Ave. #923
Riverside, CA 92504
951-741-7651 | *fax* 951-848-9426
info@blackpennypress.com
www.BlackPennyPress.com

Publisher's Cataloguing-in-Publication

Austin, Abrendal.

On a clear day you can see L.A. : a novel / Abrendal Austin. — 1st ed. — Los Angeles, CA : Black Penny Press, 2008.

p. ; cm.

ISBN: 978-0-9748066-9-3
Second in the series of Angela Jones novels that began with "A fugitive's wife".
Summary: Angela returns home to Los Angeles to visit her mother. When circumstances around Rose's death become suspicious, things start falling apart— an exiting husband, an entering fiance and the unsettling appearance of a person from her past— putting her new confidence as an independent woman to the test.

1. African American women—Fiction. 2. Self-reliance—Fiction. I. Title.

PS3601.U885 O523 2008   2007904999
813.6—dc22   0802

Printed and bound in the United States of America

Book Consultant and Shepherd: Ellen Reid www.bookshep.com
Cover Design: Dotti Albertine
Book Design: Ghislain Viau

On a Clear Day You Can See L.A.

A NOVEL

Angela sought a better future. But she was about to discover her past.

ABRENDAL AUSTIN

BLACK PENNY PRESS
RIVERSIDE, CA

Dedication

I dedicate this second novel to whoever is holding these pages right now and all the friends family and fans who helped me along the way. There are too, too many to mention and still keep my sanity. A certain sentiment goes with gratitude and I send it to you because I was fortunate enough to have you on my journey .

How wonderful it might have been for Adam and Eve to dwell in the garden with their own special family, but God knew they needed more so he created a whole world of fascinating people just like you. Keep the dream, fight the power, help the poor, embrace the rich, pick the daisies, plant the seeds, be beautiful, don't hate, respect your elders and call your mother!

In loving memory of my mother, Elizabeth Dillard.

Acknowledgments

Many thanks to my brilliant Book Shepherd, Ellen Reid, for going another round with me and for developing a marvelous team once again.

To Dotti Albertine, Patricia Bacall, Laren Bright, Ghislain Viau, and Melanie Rigney. You are all wonderful!

Prologue

Good and bad folks

IN GOOD OL' CALI (CALIFORNIA, THAT IS) there's this place called Los Angeles (L.A. for short) and there were two kinds of people back there around 1974, 1975. You was either good people or trifling people because according to the Good Book you can't be on the fence.

Now the first group of folks, the good people, went to church every Sunday morning unless they was sick or couldn't get off work. Or like in some cases, your husband gave you a black eye and you was shamed to go. The good folks also went to work for a living and gave the boss an honest day's labor. The children went to school dressed nice with their hair cut, combed, or ribboned up. And everybody looked after the neighbors' houses and kids and made sure they didn't run in the streets or get beat up too bad by the bully named Goonie from round the corner.

The good folks paid their car note and rent on time and their utilities and phones were always on. They planted brightly colored petunias, red azalea bushes and a rainbow of roses all along their nicely painted wooden fences. Some of them went to Venice Beach and played ball in the sand and didn't even care about the half-naked girls' booties in the skimpy bikinis. They believed in a little tiny look but no touching. But the trifling people did a whole lot of looking and some touching. And the good women didn't even care about the bronzed hunks all oiled down walking or posing with their muscles flexed. No cheating and no lusting was going on with the good folks in L.A.

Now the trifling folks always kept them a little something extra on the side, even if that person on the side was just as crazy as the person you had at home. You just did it because your friends did it.

Let's see what happens when the bad folks catch up with the good people. First of all back in that time, when the good folks came home from work, their furniture could be missing. The marijuana plants that they planted (for medicinal purposes) in the backyard could be gone. If they grew them in a pot, the pot would still be there but the plants pulled right out before they could get a chance to even sample it. The trifling folks even had the courage to plant some weed in the nearby church's backyard 'cause they never cut their grass and there was a lot of tall bushes anyhow. It was rumored that when the good church decided to hire a gardener, he cut the grass and stopped right at the two-foot marijuana plants. However, when the trifling person who planted it saw this he swooped up his green plants real quick and jumped back over the fence. "What a blessing that I was able to save them," he said to himself.

Another time the good met the bad was when little Jimmie was getting beat up by Goonie and his friends. Miss Julie came outside and broke it all up. Goonie went home and told his mama and his mama came back with her sister and beat up Miss Julie. In the heart of L.A. where I used to live it could get mean in those days. The good people and the bad people didn't mind loaning you a cup of sugar, some music for a birthday party, walking your kid to school, helping you fix your car, sharing a wine cooler on the porch at night or a joint first thing in the morning. In between that joint in the morning and that cooler at night those good and bad folks functioned together as well as apart but they all taught about hopes, dreams and aspirations in this wonderful thing we call LIFE.

Chapter 1

THE TRAIN STOPPED IN SAN DIEGO at three in the morning and most of the passengers were asleep, including Candi in the seat between Angela and her new friend Viola. Viola had also boarded the train in Valdosta, and she and Candi took a liking to each other right away. It was like they had known each other for some time. Their new friend was kinda plump with a round, shiny face, and Angela guessed her to be old enough to be her mother. She was well-dressed and smelled like jasmine. The conductor announced a thirty-minute delay and all who wanted to get off and re-board could do so as long as they showed their ticket stubs again.

Viola yawned and stretched her short legs. "I would get off but I'm not sure I want to do any walking just yet. I can't walk too fast since I broke my right foot. I'd mess around and miss the train and my grandchildren would not understand. You go on, get some exercise. Candi be all right sleeping right here next to me."

Angela really wanted to look around just a little and she hated sitting still too long. She got up, squeezed by Viola's knees and had leaned down to kiss Candi when Viola quietly shooed her away. Angela slowly started up the aisle and quickly turned around and held up both hands and mouthed the words "Ten minutes." Viola nodded her head then put her hand on Candi's shoulder and leaned back with her eyes closed.

Angela made her way to a magazine rack and started glancing through the *Ebony* magazine article on how to dress for the city you are in. She looked down at her black lace boots and wondered if they were out of place for the city she was going to, the city she was in now or the city she just left. Now, she thought, my leather purse might work but it is a little small. She hated big purses. They always made her look smaller than her five-foot-two frame.

There were three people in line at the counter waiting to buy tickets to Los Angeles. She kept glancing back at the train and she could see Viola nodding at her letting her know that everything was okay on board. Angela heard feet shuffling behind her. She turned around and saw a lady dressed in a torn red coat approaching her. Her black eyes were so small Angela wondered how she could see. Also, they were bloodshot, matching her outfit.

Even with air-conditioning Angela detected the scent of days-old dirt and sweat. The stranger opened her ruby mouth showing brown crooked teeth and barely uttered, "Let me, Pusha, all-knowing, tell your future for just five dollars."

Angela looked in disbelief at Pusha's black velvet turban sprinkled with tiny silver stars and certainly thought this could be a fortune-teller. She remembered Candi. "I have to get back to the train!"

Angela turned and hurried toward the train. The woman called after her, "Go on, run away from your destiny." She raised her hands in the air, raising and lowering her head, shouting, "For your uncaring soul, the curse of the gods be upon you!" Pusha continued waving her hands. "Curses! Curses! On all that you touch!" Her belly shook with laughter as Angela hurried onto the train.

Angela finally found her seat, held her child and looked out the window to see Pusha approaching someone else.

Viola laughed out loud. "Honey, I know you wanted to see San Diego, but I guess you satisfied now." The laughter ceased when Angela didn't share the humor. "Just say your prayers, child, 'cause you know that crazy woman has nothing to do with the God we serve. She just wanted to make a quick dollar." Viola closed her eyes and muttered, "I guess we in California now."

Angela remained silent and wondered what was ahead of her and why she was always so fucking curious. She fluffed the pillow under her head and was about to close her eyes when a well-dressed young Chinese man came toward Angela and Viola's row with a large green envelope in his right hand. He stopped, looked at Angela and courteously bowed his head. "Excuse me, Miss Jones, I bring for you important news." He handed her the envelope. "You must read before train goes."

Chapter 2

"*THANK* YOU. WHO IS IT FROM? There's no name on it. You sure it's for me?"

"Oh yes ma'am. It for you. Hop Sing don't know where it from. He just say give to you." He looked at Angela who barely held on to the green envelope, a puzzled look on her face. "All I can say is it was a—" Suddenly he stopped, turned his head and looked out of the window. "Oh, thank you ma'am, thank you." He left the train and ran down the platform until he was out of sight.

Viola let out a sigh as she crossed her arms over her round chest. "I bet you a thousand dollars it's from that husband of yours. You said he was good about writing make-up letters and notes. Open it up before the train pulls off because it must be something you really need to see. And I'm sure that Chinaman was 'bout to tell you too but he musta been scared. Why would he be scared? What would scare him? Oh Lord! Something tells me this is not going to be the average black women's trip to L.A. It sounds spooky to me."

Angela looked sideways at Viola and sighed. "Stick with me ol' wise chocolate travel buddy. You are in store for a most interesting ride. Did you know on a clear day you can see L.A. and all its splendor? Let's see what kind of day we find when we get there."

"All I know is I want to find a bed and sleep for a while. Then I can get up and look around and see what kind of day it is in that wicked city. Los Angeles is kinda wicked you know."

"Yeah. Wicked and sweet. Like what's probably in this envelope."

Angela continued. "You know what? I'm not falling for it this time. Pearce does go out of his way to fix his shit, but it ain't happening this time. Envelope or no envelope, he can kiss my emancipated ass. That's right. Free!"

"Whoa," said Viola, "there must have been something mighty good about him for you to marry him and stay with him all that time."

Angela smiled. "I'll tell you what was good about Pearce. He was such a gentleman. Dark chocolate face, big brown eyes with a great heart-shaped smile. Pretty boy. Handsome and real respectful. Gave me roses and perfume. And most of all, he was fabulous at lying and cheating!"

Viola sighed. "I guess it's hard to be faithful in this world with temptation everywhere. Okay, that takes care of that rascal. Now, what are you gonna do? I haven't known you that long but I know good and well you gone open that envelope. You're too curious. It could be some money, or some jewelry. Let me shake it."

"Here, shake it but don't open it. I'm not looking in it now. That Pusha lady said she put a curse on my life and this envelope probably is the beginning of it."

Viola shook the envelope and it sounded like paper inside. "Well…It is yours and it is a big key to your future."

"Or to my past. Either way there's a time and place for everything and this junk can be opened at another time."

Viola looked at her and said, "Hmm. Okay. It's your life."

"Viola, I gave Pearce plenty of chances. I went with him to Georgia and he cheated on me. Even after I left my own family to run away from the law with him because he said he was framed for that robbery. I'm tired of it all now. Me and my baby need us a break. I even had a nice-looking white man who was so good to me and Candi and then Pearce came back and ruined that."

Viola looked at her with a gleam in her eye and said, "So you had somebody too. A white man in Georgia?"

"Yeah, I said *white man in Georgia*. Carl is his name. He's an attorney—a little older than me but he's fine with green eyes and always smells nice. He's not perfect but he treated me better than—never mind, I'm just tired. I want my own life now. My family was worried about me. I'm glad I'm going home again. I really do miss my momma." She leaned back in the seat back and closed her eyes.

The announcement came that no one wanted to hear. "Ladies and gentlemen, I'm sorry but we have a minor change in our schedule because of bad weather. Train number 455 connecting from Chicago is delayed and we have to wait for them. We're sorry for the inconvenience but we should be leaving in an hour which will be five a.m. Those of you who wish to get off can do so and re-board. Just keep your ticket stubs. We have some complimentary coupons for you at the Froggy Hop Café on the adjacent pier. The food is excellent, the service is top quality. They also serve breakfast twenty-four hours and the clam chowder on the seafood menu is said to be the best in Southern California. Again, we apologize for any inconvenience."

Viola said, "I want to get off this time for sure and call my son and grandchildren. I'll tell them just to wait for my call when we arrive and don't worry about sitting in that drafty Union Station. In all my years of traveling I know one thing for sure. And that is things happen and trips get delayed. I'll just call 'em soon as we get in the restaurant because some of them bad-ass kids are probably still up watching TV at this crazy hour 'cause they don't have school tomorrow. With all this delaying, it will probably be daylight when I get to L.A. and everyone will be up already anyway. Soon as I rest up in a real bed we usually get in the street and go to a fair or get on a boat ride." She sighed and gazed out the window. "Los Angeles, California. The so-called city of angels. So close and yet so far."

Angela sighed and stood up. She started to pick up Candi who was awake now but changed her mind and let her walk. "I'm going to that café now even if it is four a.m. and see what that wonderful Southern California clam chowder is all about. After all on a train ride you can do what you want and eat what you want anytime 'cause all we been doing is resting for the last three days. The only cooking I want now is my mom's. Some turkey and dressing, fried corn, gravy, green beans. All that good stuff. I already told her what I want to eat, and you can come over too, Viola. I know you will like her. She'll be glad to tell you about how silly I was when I was younger." Angela got quiet for a minute and Viola took the conversation back.

"Your mother will be so proud of you. Why are you looking so sad? You're starting a whole new life."

"It's nothing much," she said. "That fortune-teller got me thinking, thinking, thinking…what if everything in L.A. goes wrong and I made a big mistake in leaving Georgia?"

"What if everything goes right? Wherever you are, there is a choice to make. You can be happy or sad. It's up to you. Make a choice."

"Okay, I'm okay, now let's go eat and I better not see that Pusha again even though she reminds me of my mom's oldest sister Liza. Real light skinned with long soft hair like corn silk. Froggy Hop Café, here we come! I'm sure they have a phone in there. I have to call my mom too."

When they made their way through the aisle and stepped down from the train onto the platform, it was still dark out and pretty quiet except for the white waves rolling in the baby blue ocean and a few lively birds. The chilly, salty air felt good and the small pier had five or six fishermen tying and untying their large and small vessels to the dock. Angela walked slowly, holding Candi's hand with her left hand and her beaded purse on the other shoulder. Candi held Viola's hand with her left hand. The cool air woke them up even more and reminded Angela of how early it really was.

Angela stopped at the wooden fence so Candi could see the sailboats, some seagulls standing around and some baby fish floating under the water. Candi reached into Angela's purse and took out her little rag doll, Tina, and accidentally pulled the green envelope out and it fell right into the water. No one saw it happen, and the envelope floated until it disappeared under the pier into the darkness.

Angela went ahead of the two of them. "Hey slowpokes, come on. Let's see what's to eat at this Froggy Hop place. Maybe they got some good pancakes or maybe some spicy tacos. I haven't had any good Mexican food since I left L.A. Shoot! I'm gonna put that Valdosta behind me for a while and when we get inside, I'm gonna open up that stupid envelope. Yeah, it might be a fortune in there."

Viola and Candi caught up with Angela as she stopped and held open the café door for them. Viola walked slowly through the entrance with Candi and stopped to wait for the hostess to seat them. "You brought that ol' envelope, huh? You were just buying time. I knew you were going to open it."

Angela closed the glass door. "Oh yes, you were right. I have it right here." She reached into her burgundy purse and moved everything around feeling the satin lining which was a little torn. "I don't have it now. I know I put it in here when I stuck that doll in here."

Angela gave up, resigned to the fact that the envelope was not in her purse. "Oh well, who knows? Maybe it's on the train."

They all got seated in a tiny booth and put their coupons on the shiny red table. Angela ordered oatmeal with bananas and strawberries for Candi and shrimp tacos for herself. Viola ordered the Froggy special omelet with waffles that they all would share.

Angela went to a phone booth in the corner, which was finally empty because of all the people calling their relatives about the delay. She dialed her mother, Rose.

"Hey, mom, we will be there soon. Right now we're getting ready to eat in this dumb old Froggy Hop café with some free coupons they gave us."

Rose answered kinda sleepily as if she had just woke up. "Oh Angela child, this is a dream come true having my daughter and granddaughter in California at last. I'm gonna get some more rest now. I just been real tired lately. Oh, but I gotta tell you who called here asking for you already and you ain't even here yet."

Viola could see Angela's face from where they sat. In between answering Candi's questions about all the little red and green frog decals everywhere she was trying to make out the meaning in Angela's expressions. Soon, Angela just hung up the phone and shook her head. She went back to the table and squeezed in beside Candi just as a gum-chewing Hispanic waitress set down a frosty cold goblet of orange juice and quickly turned away.

Viola asked, "Is everything all right?"

"Sure—sure it is. But you won't believe who's trying to reach me." Then she folded her arms on the table, rested her head on them and started crying uncontrollably.

Chapter 3

ON THE OTHER SIDE OF THE COUNTRY, back in Valdosta, Georgia, Michael Rivers (better known as Mike to all his two friends, Jamie Brown and Stella Franklin) prepared to stretch out and take a nap on the damp bank by the lake. Mike had a slim build, brown eyes, a more than cute copper face, was average height and in good shape for a forty year old man. This lunch hour he and Jamie chose to stay on the grounds at the Holiday Inn where they worked. Stella was cool most of the time but he didn't know if she would make it on time. But she would probably be there, just late, as usual which was her style.

So for now Mike had to settle for Jamie, the biggest whining bitch of a man he ever saw. All Jamie ever talked about was how his wife, Diamond, left him last week. This cool afternoon Mike and Jamie were sitting on the muddy bank at Lincoln Lake trying to catch some speckled trout, when Jamie started his daily spiel about his used-to-be better half. He moved his head from side to side.

"I'm sho glad she left. She think she messing up something with me but I ain't gotta spend another sorry-ass penny on her jacked-up Mercedes. She gonna have to learn to take care o' shit. Let her go with her good-for-nothing brother and his badass kids. She gonna get tired of them too. Yeah, you watch, she gone be back. Sho as I tell you. But what's so killing is I don't even want her fat Jell-O-shaking booty back."

Mike half-listened to Jamie, but he didn't dare interrupt 'cause he knew Jamie would grab you by the collar and push you to the ground if you disagreed with him, or if he even thought you wanted to disagree with him. Mike just didn't feel like rolling around in the dirt today. So he baited his fishing pole, propped it on the damp shore and leaned back on the smooth two-foot high tree stump that doubled for their table. Red ants were already crawling around his soda, sunglasses and pumpkin seeds trying to mess up his relaxation. He sat back up and finally answered Jamie.

"I know that's right." He chose his words carefully. "You know what, Jamie. I would just let her go. Yeah, I sure would just let her stay gone, man."

Now Jamie was about forty years old too. He looked good to a lot of people and he made sure of that because he had a big black mole that messed up his right hand. His strong features made his flawless dark face look like a sculptured African warrior.

He kept his head bald except for a neatly trimmed letter J on his left temple and a D for his wife on the right temple. His straight teeth shone like white marble. He didn't like fishing but he went with Mike 'cause nobody wanted to hang around with him. They just didn't understand him.

He held up his brown Thermos. "Let's drink to that fat cow being gone."

Mike picked up his cola and tapped it on the Thermos. "Yeah, let's drink to that fat cow being gone." He reached down to check his pole and suddenly Jamie shoved him onto the gray mud.

"Are you sure? Are you really glad she's gone?" Jamie yelled as loud as he could even though Mike was about three feet away. "You better not be lying, motherfucker. I know you be lying to me sometime. You better be glad she's gone!"

Mike pushed Jamie away and got up, gathered his things quickly and walked away, shaking his head. "I don't know why I fool with that fool. That's it. He can't go with me no more. No more. I mean no more!" He put his tackle in the back of his Chevy pickup, got in, locked the door and rolled down the window just a bit. He spread the old green towel on the long seat and fell asleep.

A few minutes later he woke to a knock on the window and looked up. Jamie stood there smiling, the sparkle from his gold tooth hitting Mike in the face.

"Here comes Stella, man. She's coming right now!"

Damn, he better not be lying just to get back in good with me. Mike sat up, blinked his eyes, and then couldn't move anymore. Sure enough, coming this way was his other crazy friend, Stella. And she looked beautiful as always. Maybe even more so today.

Jamie knocked on the truck door. "Let me in, man."

Mike unlocked the door, forgetting he wasn't talking to Jamie anymore. In fact he forgot everything right now. Nothing mattered but Stella.

They never knew her real age but guessed she was about thirty-five. Today Stella wore a light yellow sundress which came off her thin sunburned pink shoulders. Her whole body was slim. Just straight up and down. She had a yellow and brown silk shawl around her, and a wide-brimmed, peach-colored straw hat shaded her eyes. Her skinny black heels brought her closer and closer.

Stella's face lit up like an angel. Her long red hair blew in the wind, making her look like she walked in slow motion. She stopped, put her left hand on her hip, and swung the shawl over her shoulder.

They looked at her from their position in the truck. Mike sighed. "We might as well get out. I guess she decided she could join us today after all and she might have something special for us but she ain't gone come any closer. If we wanna see what she got, we have to get out of this here truck."

Jamie hit the dashboard lightly with his right fist. "Dang, man. You know she don't play fair. She always tricks us. Just 'cause she cute don't mean we got to talk to her. Diamond said she don't want me talking to Stella no more anyhow because she's white and she thinks she's better than anybody else. And Diamond says she wants everybody to do her work for her while she flirts with every man she sees. And she don't care if they married or not and when we have potlucks she always bringing that stupid old tea from her momma way over there in Germany like nobody ever had any tea before. And Diamond says…"

Mike reached out put his hand in front of Jamie's mouth. "Okay! Enough already!"

Jamie looked at Mike and said quietly, "I'm sorry, man. Diamond's not important anymore because she left and that's that." Then he perked up and smiled. "Diamond's gone and I can do what I want to now. I'm free at last."

Mike put his hand on the door handle. "You coming, man? It's now or never. You know she not gonna leave until we come out."

Jamie sighed and checked his appearance in the mirror. "I'm ready and Diamond is just gonna have to kill me. Damn. She gonna kill me!"

They both got out at the same time and walked slowly toward Stella. Her straight face turned into an impish grin when she saw them get out of the car. When they reached her she held them both briefly around the waist. "Oh my. How are my two favorite men in the whole world? You gentlemen look just charming today. We're gonna have a fabulous time today at our tea party. My darling mother sent us some tea all the way from Germany."

Jamie and Mike looked at each other, still not trusting her. Mike perked up and rubbed his hands together. "Okay," he said. "Let's go back to our stump—excuse me, I mean our marble table."

Jamie spread the red tablecloth on the tree stump and set out three white porcelain cups and three blue linen napkins. Stella gave him the tiny portable teapot and lay down on the thick grass and put her feet up on the tree trunk, letting her dress fall down showing all her shapely legs and thighs and stopping just before exposing her panties.

"Hey guys, where would you all go if you all could go anywhere in the world?"

Mike poured the hot orange tea like he always did. This new blend had a mild cinnamon aroma. It looked all right to him but he still didn't trust that Stella. He said, "I want to go to New York City, New York. I want to go up in the Statue of Liberty and look over the whole city."

Jamie joined in. "You gonna take your wife with you?"

"Yeah, but I'll let her go shopping 'cause she don't like heights and that way I can look at all the pretty women I want to."

They were approached by a light-skinned middle-aged black man in a yellow polo shirt and trousers, kinda heavy round the middle, with an assortment of silver and blue rings on every finger. Jamie thought to himself, *It's some guy Stella is going out with coming to talk shit to us when all we're doing is having fun.*

The stranger said, "I'm looking for Pearce Jones. I hear he works here. Or his wife, Angela."

Stella answered, "We don't know of those two people at all." She looked at Mike. "Do we?"

Mike shook his head. "Oh hell no. We don't know anybody by that name."

The stranger stood holding his head down and blinked his eyes as if he was trying not to cry.

Jamie said, "And what do you want with Pearce and Angela anyway even if we did know them?"

"My name is Tom Adams. I'm Angela's father and I came to right some wrongs. I need to find my daughter. I'm getting too old and I need to see my only girl. I don't know if I can tell you all why. I heard from some good sources that you all might know them. You all look like nice people and all but how do I know I can trust you? I have something to give her in this envelope."

He held onto it with his arms folded across it as if to shield it from their curious eyes. The three of them all sat down on a bench as if on cue like they had all day for this Tom Adams to find a way to trust them. They remained silent and let him stand there. Stella finally spoke in her soft sexy voice. "We have all been working here at this Inn for at least five years. People come from far and wide."

Jamie interrupted, "From all around the world…"

Mike lay back on the bench behind Jamie and Stella. "Europe, Africa, Saudi Arabia and Brooklyn."

Jamie continued, "Willie Nelson just stayed here last week. He always comes here when he's in town. Ray Charles brings his whole family here sometimes. Sons, daughters and all them babies."

Stella slowly held out her hand. "Let me take care of that special envelope for a very special father." Tom gave it to her. She placed it gently in her brown burlap tote bag. "I heard about some new guy named Pearce. I'll see that his wife—you said Angela?"

"Yeah, Angela."

She smiled at him with her cute pink lips. "I'll see she gets it. That's all I can say and it won't take too long. A couple of days maybe."

Tom looked her straight in the eyes now, taking his eyes off those lips. He said slowly as if to make her understand, "It really needs to go to Angela. If you lose it you lose a part of my soul. It is crucial and here's six hundred dollars down payment for you all and all your trouble. When I know she has it then you get the other half. Six hundred more dollars." He handed them six crisp new hundred dollar bills.

Mike looked at Stella as she folded up the bills in her hand. "Tom, how do we get in touch with you?"

Tom said, "Don't you worry about reaching me, you just worry about reaching my girl. I'll know she got it." He went on back up the hill to his brand new tan-colored Cadillac with whitewalls and shiny chrome rims.

Mike said, "He looks like a gangster to me with all that silver. I don't trust nobody with all that cash on 'em. We'll call Hop Sing. He will know what to do."

Jamie said, "Where's Stella going with our money? She know she was supposed to split that three ways."

Mike said, "Dang. She got us again."

Jamie turned around as Stella started to run up the slight hill back to the Holiday Inn where they all worked. "Hey, where you going with our money? We're supposed to split that three ways."

Stella stopped for a moment. "I gotta get the dinner trays set up. No problem. I'll catch you all tomorrow. Hop Sing's in town. I'll give the envelope to him tonight. Don't worry guys. I love you." Jamie and Mike watched her go inside the Inn and close the door. "Dang," Mike said as he grabbed the cups from their table. "She always gets us."

Jamie said as he helped clean up, "Yeah, she got us again. I could use that two hundred now, man. But we'll get her next time. Don't worry man, we'll get her. We should not have trusted her anyway and we know she ain't gonna give us no money."

Mike said, "Yeah, it's worth two hundred dollars for her to leave us alone."

Jamie continued, "I wonder how Hop Sing is gonna find Angela. I heard she finally left that Pearce. Took the baby, the clothes, furniture and everything and split. He ain't got nothing but the car. Sometimes you get tired of mess. That's why I don't care if Diamond comes back or not."

Mike said quickly, "Gotta go. See ya later man." He was not about to have that conversation with Jamie again today. He went on back in the Inn to his accounting duties.

Meanwhile Jamie sat down by himself on the tree stump and looked around at all the giant magnolia trees and flowerbeds that he kept so neat at this place. He got up and put on his goggles, ready to trim some orange azalea bushes. Then he snatched them right off and sat back down. He hesitated for a few seconds, then he looked up at the light blue sky and said, "Dear Lord, please bring back my wife, Diamond. I'll treat her good this time. Amen."

Chapter 4

HOP S<small>ING WRAPPED HIS STIFF FINGERS</small> around his steaming hot cup of spearmint tea, placed it under his nose and took a deep breath and woke up a little more. He checked the supplies in his briefcase one more time before heading to the airport. He had his alarm clock, calculator, folders and pictures of his petit-sized brothers from his homeland, China. He just had to put in the mysterious envelope he would have to get someone to deliver for him, or worst case do it himself. All he knew about it was that a sharp-looking, sad-looking man gave Diamond, his cook, two hundred dollars to get it to the man's daughter. She had left it for him with a note saying it was for some woman named Angela who would be on a train in San Diego. Diamond had somehow tracked down the train's arrival time in San Diego.

It was damn early, but he was flying to the West Coast anyway, so he guessed he could do a good deed for the poor guy. He briefly wondered why Diamond had been so adamant about not saying anything to Pearce about it. Hop Sing shook his head. It was none of his business and it sounded pretty spooky anyway. He put his mind back into how he was going to renovate his larger Inn in San Diego, California.

He'd opened this cozy little Holiday Inn in Valdosta four years ago. Money being tight at that time, he hired Pearce because he liked his attitude, he worked cheap and didn't ask for much. All his references had checked out so he let him run the front desk even though he suspected something odd was going on with him. But then he figured everybody had something odd going on with them. Anyhow, he was a good worker and this week he would leave him in charge again.

"Pearce, you be okay? Ten day a long time. It no problem for you?"

Pearce sat in the office chair behind the mahogany counter and twisted it from side to side a little bit and stopped. He sighed. "Okay, boss man. Just listen. This is what is going to happen. You are going to California today and I'll be just fine right here. Don't worry. Have I ever let you down? No. Looks like you got everything and there's the taxi. Let me help you."

Pearce carried Hop Sing's burgundy leather suitcase and put it into the taxi for him and shut the door. He walked slowly back into the lobby and saw a green envelope on the counter. He raced outside and was able to catch up with the orange taxi since it was going slowly into the busy street. Hop Sing rolled down the window. Pearce said, out of breath, "Here, you left this. Don't you need it? It sure is taped up good. Whatever it is they don't want nobody peeking in that!"

"Yeah," Hop Sing said before he rolled the window back up, blocking out the heat and humidity. "It for somebody daughter."

Pearce walked back inside and fixed the counter up like he wanted it. After all he was running this place now and for the next ten days he would call the shots around here. He put pictures of his wife, Angela, and daughter, Candi, right on the shelf next to his California coffee mug. He then sat down and leaned back in the office chair with his feet propped up on the counter and lit a cigarette. He thought, Yeah, Mr. Hop Sing, go on and have a good time in California 'cause when you come back I'm going out there myself to get my good old wife and child.

He sat up and took the silver picture frame in both hands and said out loud, "You know you still love me, Angela. I'll give you time to let off some steam and then I got plans for us. Ten days and counting."

Chapter 5

VIOLA JUST LOOKED AT ANGELA and held Candi's hand. She knew Candi was going to start crying soon. Just seeing her mama cry like that would be hard on any child. "Okay, Angela," she said softly, "you have to tell me something. Who is looking for you?"

Angela straightened up and wiped her eyes with the soft white napkin from the table. "Okay, this might seem silly, but it's Pearce and I know I said I didn't want anything to do with him, but he says he's going to turn himself in for Candi's sake. He just wants to see me first so we can get everything straightened out before they lock him up." She paused and sighed. "I never thought he'd do it, but he called my mom's house. And that's a first for him. He's coming to see me soon. He told my mom he's serious this time."

Viola shook her head just a tiny bit. "Honey, you know he can do all of that without you. Right? You don't have to see him, Angela. Is that envelope from him?"

"Could be, I suppose."

Viola frowned. "I don't know about all this. You sure you can take it? You went through too much. And Candi don't need anymore foolishness."

Angela looked at her plate as Viola poured milk into Candi's oatmeal and stirred it up for her, then ate her eggs real slow. Viola decided to stop asking Angela about Pearce right now.

They finished eating and went back toward the train. Angela said, "Isn't it nice and fresh out here ? The ocean air is so salty." They boarded the train and one of the porters approached them after they sat down. "Excuse me, ladies, but you all lost this. Someone saw you drop it in the water and brought it to the train for you." He touched it lightly to see if it was still wet. "This must be one of them really waterproof envelopes. Whatever's in there must be real important. Ma'am." He nodded his head and hurried on back up the aisle. Angela thanked him and Candi said, "Mommie, can I open it? Let me open it, Mommie. I hope it's a picture of my daddy. I wanna see my daddy!"

"Oh Viola, you see what I mean. She wants her daddy. If only it was just me to think about…" Angela held the envelope close to her chest. Just then she glanced out the window and saw Pusha, the fortune-teller, sitting on a bench looking real tired and staring right at their window. "I'll be right back. Right back. Then we open the mystery envelope. Right back." Angela hurried over to the bench where Pusha sat and then she stopped. Suddenly she felt a bit of pity for this decrepit looking soul.

Pusha patted the space beside her. "Please sit down, young lady. I have words for you."

Angela reached into her denim jacket and took out a twenty dollar bill. "This is for you. Buy yourself something pretty with it. Maybe a new hat. We all could use a new hat!"

Pusha laughed, showing her brown teeth. "You thought there was a curse on you. You know I don't have that power. But just in case I did, I'm taking it off right now. And may your days be prosperous and beautiful." She started to shake a little and tears were in her slanted little eyes. "I can tell you are a good girl. Don't you let nobody make you crazy like me. Take care of yourself. That's important! Then you can take care of other people."

Angela hugged her and started to cry.

After a moment, Pusha shoved her away. "Go on. The world is waiting for you. Live a good life and find something to be happy about every day. And don't forget to pray for your old friend Pusha, too."

Right then Pusha turned to a lady walking by with two small children and said in a whisper, "Hey, come here, I got something to tell you for just five dollars." But she looked tired. Angela laughed and climbed back onto the train. She sat down with Candi and Viola again.

Angela helped Candi get comfortable with her doll and then she leaned into the seat and closed her eyes and spoke very softly as if she were in a different place. "I wish everybody would leave me alone. Maybe they will if I open the darn envelope. It seems like the whole world is waiting."

She took a pencil from her purse and carefully sliced the damp envelope open at the top. A glossy five-by-seven-inch black-and-white photo was way down in there, stuck in the crease. She pulled it out. Viola and Candi looked on silently. It was a man; her mother, Rose; and a little girl about two years old and a small boy a little bigger than the girl. He had his head turned sideways and he was looking down at the ground so you couldn't really make out who he was unless you already knew. Angela turned the picture over. It said, *To my sweet daughter from Tom, your daddy. Call me soon as you get this. Don't be mad. Please let me explain. There are things you need to know and only I can tell you the truth. Call this number. I have always loved you.*

Viola said real soft and slow, "Your daddy. Wow. So it was a man after you."

Angela said, "Heck no." Then she started to crumple up the picture.

Viola grabbed her hand. "Stop. Don't you think you should think about that for a bit?"

"Yeah. All I need is some more drama now. I left that stuff back in Georgia. Oh my God. I can't take it. Don't want to deal with this now. What am I supposed to do?"

"Look," said Viola. "If you stop and wallow in this now, you will drive yourself crazy. You have faith and faith got you this far. If I were you, I would handle it now and get it over with. If you want, I'll watch the baby." Viola stood up and took Candi's hand in hers and waited.

Angela looked at Viola with surprise. "Why do you want me to call somebody I don't even know? Just because he is my father who I have not seen in a million years."

Viola sat back down halfway in the seat still ready to get up at any second. "Wasn't that saga you been through all about a father being away from his family? Your husband's father was taken away to jail and spent too much time away from his wife and children. Didn't you say Pearce took your child away from you for awhile because of the daddy thing? This man who says he is your dad has got to have something good to tell you."

Angela went back inside the Froggy Hop Café and called the number on the picture. As the phone rang Angela's heart started to beat faster. What would she say to a man who she hadn't seen for years, who had missed every important event in her young life, who…the phone stopped ringing and a man's smooth baritone voice said, "Hello."

Angela took a deep breath and said to herself, *Oh dear God. Help me.*

The voice said hello again but this time in a very patient friendly tone as though he was waiting for someone special to call.

Angela finally spoke softly almost in a whisper. "Are you my father?"

"Angela. I knew you would call. I remember your voice like it was yesterday. I have been praying that you were okay. I am so sorry to have been away from you so long. Where are you, baby? I want to see you. I need to make it all right with us again."

"Daddy, I don't have much time. I'm in San Diego waiting for the train on into L.A. It should be leaving in a few minutes. I'll be at Mom's in a couple of hours. My little girl is with me too."

"Okay," he said. "I know you have to go, baby. Your mama still stay with her sister Mazie?"

"Yeah, them two are still very close. They can't do nothing without each other. What do you have to tell me? What about that picture? Who is that little boy?"

She heard him sigh on the other end of the phone. "Angela. My Angela, I was hoping I could tell you all of it in person, but I made a promise to myself that if I ever got the chance I would tell you. I didn't want your mama to know years ago that I had another child a little older than you. She thought that kid in the photo was my sister's boy. I lost track of him and his mama years ago. I messed up and wasn't 'round him either."

"My brother. Okay, so you made that plain. Where is he now?"

"California is where he was born but I heard he went down south to Georgia somewhere. We called him Junior."

Chapter 6

WHEN Angela got to the train station in Los Angeles her mother wasn't at there to meet her and Candi. "Oh gosh! Something has to be wrong." She had no choice but to call her mom's house. "Hey Mazie," she asked her auntie who answered on the first ring, "where is Mama? How come she's not here? I told her we would be late."

"Angela honey, I'm sorry to blurt this out to you, your mom is in the hospital. Right after you called, she started having a little trouble breathing. I think it's okay, probably just the excitement of seeing you, but we didn't take any chances so we went to the hospital. I'm sure it's nothing. I had to stay here to wait for you 'cause I didn't want to leave and miss you all. She is okay though, just some cold. You know Rose liked to smoke and that cigarette cough got to her. Stay right there. I'll bring the car right now."

Viola called her family and told them what happened and to pick her up at St. John's hospital on Crenshaw. She went with Angela to take care of Candi while Angela visited her mom with her aunt Mazie.

Angela left Candi in the waiting area with Viola and Mazie, her mom's older sister, and hurried to her mother's hospital room. Angela stopped, peeked into the room and walked in slowly, bewildered by what she saw. Her mom had an oxygen mask on and an IV, a blood pressure cuff and a pulse oximeter taped to her index finger. Angela walked over to the bed, took Rose's skinny hand in hers, leaned down and kissed her forehead. "I love you mama. You are going to be all right." There was a big change in her mom since the last time she had seen her when she had come to Valdosta to see them last year. She had lost about twenty pounds. A dark blue turban covered her head and Angela noticed her thick hair had thinned out quite a bit. She thought she was seeing things. She could not believe this was her mother lying in front of her, helpless.

Angela thought to herself, *Oh my God. Did I cause all this because I ran away with Pearce? Was she so worried about me that she got sick?*

Rose looked at her daughter with sad, weak eyes and tried to take the mask off. She mumbled something under it. "Take me home now. I don't want to be here."

Angela grabbed her hand. "No you don't, lady. You need to wear that for awhile."

Just then a too-slender black nurse came in. "Hi, are you her family? I'm Julie and if you have any questions I can answer them for you as soon as I give her meds."

Angela answered, "I'm her daughter, Angela. I just came from Georgia on the train and I find her in here." Then she moved back out of the way and sat in a nearby chair and watched as Julie changed the IV fluids and gave Rose some meds through her IV.

Angela waited patiently for the nurse to finish checking her mom and then followed her outside where she was writing her notes. "What happened? How long is she going to be here?"

"Angela, she is very, very sick. Her O_2 is too low and we need to get her hemoglobin increased. She has pneumonia-like symptoms but the doctor has ordered a biopsy of her lungs. There was some kind of spot on the radiology report. We'll know more tomorrow."

Angela sat down in a nearby chair, overwhelmed with fatigue and disbelief. She knew the nurse was only doing her job and could work no miracles for her mom. She could only follow doctor's orders. She said in a small voice, "Can I bring her something? What can I do?"

"You can be strong for her and encourage her to take fluids and eat. She seems to have given up the will to get better." With that nurse Julie walked on out of the room.

The next morning they took Rose to intensive care and hooked her up to the ventilator for awhile.

Angela knew for sure that this was not what her mom would want so she went to see Dr. Henry at his office the next day. She didn't want to talk to him on the hospital unit. She figured what she had to say would have more impact in a different setting. She waited in the foyer until the nurse told her she could see the doctor.

Dr. Henry was average height, about five foot ten. His brown hair, which matched the few freckles on his pinkish face, was wavy and cut very close to his head in an unusual style for a professional white man. He had taken his white coat off and it lay across the desk real close to him because he might need it any minute to go back to work, but he kept his big black stethoscope around his neck.

Angela knew him very well many years ago, and now looking at him reminded her of another place and time where she had last seen him. He sat with his back to her, looking out of the bay window.

She stood there behind him. "Alex" was all she could say.

"I knew you would come here to see me, Angela, even though there are a lot of doctors on your mother's case now."

Angela started to cry. "Alex, you have to do something. You can't let her die. You knew her too a long time ago. She took care of you and your brother. Your whole family!"

He turned around and looked at her. Tears rolled down his pink tan cheeks, but he had to be a doctor right now. "I'm sorry but your mother has lung cancer." He paused, giving her time to process this news. He went on when she didn't reply. "We have to start chemotherapy right away. Of course we will give her all the support and preliminary meds to help control the nausea. If she were a little bit stronger she would have a better chance.

Right now we can give her a fifty-fifty chance of survival and remission. I don't know if I can remain on this case."

Angela knew Dr. Henry because her mom used to clean his parents' house before he even went to med school. She had a lot of respect for him but this time she did not like him telling it straight up like it was. "Dr. Henry, I cannot have my mama suffering like that. I know she is intubated but she is making it very plain to me and my aunt that she wants no part of the ventilator."

"Damn it! Angela. She was like a mother to me. My parents were gone so much that sometimes I thought Rose was my mother! And now I am a responsible doctor." He flipped through his notes regarding Rose. "There are no special orders to cease life support at any time. We have to do all we can. Angela, where is your father? I know he was gone from your life when you were a teenager. Is he anywhere around? He is the only one who can reverse any orders. Go get him."

Angela said, "I want her off that horrible thing. She would not let me suffer like that. I know she wouldn't."

"Angela, I have other patients to see. Can we continue this conversation later? There is still a chance." He stood up. She kept asking and he shook his head. "Talk to me in the morning. Go get some rest and find that father of yours too, Angela. There's always hope. Miracles do happen." He held her hand briefly, keeping his professionalism intact.

Angela went to the chapel and lit two of the skinny yellow candles. It was quiet and dark except for the white flames. Two other people sat in the pew on the other side of the small chapel. The violins from Beethoven's Eighth Symphony played and

Angela wondered why someone would want to listen to that in a chapel where people were sad. The melody went up and down. She sat down and remembered all the times she and Pearce had been in her mother's house. In her kitchen and in her huge back-yard and even the crazy way she always told them what to do even though they never asked her opinion. And Angela realized now how right Rose had been about her leaving California with him to escape justice from his crime. *Oh God,* Angela thought. *I have to call our friends Buster and Dixie Mae in Georgia so they can pray for her.*

Angela lay down on the red cushion on the brown lacquered pew which was rubbed well with orange furniture polish, and fell into a restless slumber. She kept waking up during the evening but couldn't move. It was as if something had her tied down. She tried to move her arms and legs but nothing happened. Not so much as a tiny little finger could she move. Her mind continued to drift in and out of awareness but her whole body seemed to sink right through the pew into a deep, deep black hole until she felt something touch her. She woke up and after realizing where she was she sat with her face in her hands and whispered, "Take me. Take me, God. Don't let my mama suffer anymore. Take me. Let me die, let me die."

Dr. Henry had stood watching Angela sleeping through the window in the chapel door. He opened the door slightly for a moment and heard Angela calling on God. He thought about her innocence and how she had helped so much when he was crying over his girlfriend while they were in high school. So much time had passed since then but he could never ever forget

Angela and her mom. It was clear in his mind like it had happened yesterday. And sometimes he wondered if it had really happened.

Alex Henry had always wanted to become a doctor like his father. His then-girlfriend had just called him and said he was too boring and she wanted more excitement and they could be friends, two days before his final exams. Angela and her mom were staying with him and his brother while his parents were on a skiing trip in Big Bear. Rose kept their house clean for them during the day but this weekend Angela came along with her to stay with the boys.

Rose was asleep in the upstairs guest suite. Angela came quietly downstairs in her pink satin robe and flannel pajamas. He sat in the side chair and looked out of the oval window at the dark quiet lake across the lane and the giant green palm leaves as they moved gently in the slight winter breeze. The five foot tall oak grandfather clock had just struck midnight and continued serenading the split-level house with the side-to-side movement of the brass pendulum inside. Swish, swish.

Angela's vanilla fragrance announced her entrance. He continued staring out the window knowing that he should turn to greet her. He welcomed her and resented her at the same time because she would be invading his feelings and his feelings were too fragile now to share them with anyone. All he could do was think about his ex-girl and how he wanted to do nothing and he would do just that for the rest of his life. Forget finals. Forget being a doctor right now.

She gently touched his right shoulder. "Alex, Barbara's not the only girl. My Mom told me what happened. That's really why

I came for the weekend. To kinda check on you I guess. You can't sit around and do nothing. Please take your final exams. Even you can't afford a failing grade, honor student. Your parents are depending on you. We all are."

"I don't care about them either. I'm done. I'm done. I'm not doing anything."

She sighed. "For goodness' sakes. Then do it for me."

He looked at her with despair. "You want me to forget everything that happened and take the finals?"

"Yes, you can do it."

"What makes you so special that you can make me take 'em?"

She sat across from him on the sofa. "I'll jump in the ice-cold pool if you promise to take them. And you know how I hate to go out in the cold."

He looked at her. "Now I would love to see that but that's not going to work either. Good try though."

She took off her robe and headed for the patio door, at the same time unbuttoning her pajama top. "How about a skinny dip?"

She took off her top then and started to remove the pants.

He stopped her with his hands holding onto hers. "As much as I would enjoy this show, I know you are not a good swimmer." They stared at each other for a moment. He spoke. "It's cold as hell out here. What are we doing?"

"Going skinny dipping." Then she grabbed his hand and pulled him with her into the cool water with all his clothes on. They went under, came up and laughing and shivering and ran into the pool house and got some big yellow towels and helped each other dry off. They flicked on the heat lamp and turned on the tea kettle.

"Are you feeling any better now? I'll make us a hot brandy drink to celebrate your taking the finals."

Alex remained silent and sat there on the sofa while Angela poured the brandy into the hot teacups and added a lemon slice to each one. They sipped in silence for a while. Alex put his feet on the center table and leaned back. "I never thought I could hurt like this. When is the pain going to stop, Angela? When will I forget?"

She turned the stereo on and Otis Redding's "Pain in my Heart" played quietly in the background. Angela began rubbing his shoulders very gently. "The pain is never going to end. It's just going to hide and even if you live to be a hundred and ten you will always remember the time Barbara broke up with you. She left you with some good memories too. It's part of what you will remember too. So many good things are ahead of you too, Alex."

She saw tears in his blue eyes and he kept blinking like he was trying to stop them. She held his hand and sat beside him. "You are so handsome, strong and smart and all the girls wish they had you." She kissed his face starting with his forehead and continued down to his warm lips, where she lingered. He opened his mouth and she found his tongue. He removed her towel and she removed his. His fingers touched her nipples and he kissed them one at a time.

She was ready for him. Her whole body was on fire with desire. She wanted to moan but she knew her mom was somewhere in the main house. She thought, *Please God, let mama be upstairs asleep.*

He placed her hands on him just where he wanted them. She massaged him and opened her lips and used her tongue again to further arouse him. When he could wait no longer he climbed on top and gently entered her. She reached on the floor and grabbed her shirt and put it in her mouth to drown out the moans from the pain of this new thing undoing her virginity. Soon she relaxed and was able to kiss him and put her tongue all over his mouth. He kissed her breasts one at a time. They made love with all the emotions they had to drown out his sorrow and pain. They continued holding, caressing and replacing his sorrow and pain with passion. She got on top and squeezed herself on him as she slid up and down. Finally they reached best climax Angela or Alex Henry ever had.

Back in reality, he scribbled on his notepad. "Consider it done. All things work together for the good for those who love God and are called according to his purpose." He opened the chapel door. She remained asleep. He touched her arm gently, wanting to wake her up, but changed his mind and stuck the note right beside her slightly underneath her small purse so she would see it when she woke up.

Angela woke up, sat up on the bench and brushed her hair in place. She picked her purse up from the bench and the note from Dr. Henry fell on the floor without her ever seeing it.

Chapter 7

LATER ON Angela sat in the waiting room close to her mother's unit. She looked out of the window at the brightly lit hospital parking lot which was packed with all kinds of people coming and going. She saw men and women of all ages, sizes and colors. Even children and babies. At the main entrance, some people hurried in and out of the automatic glass doors and some walked very, very slowly. Several patients accompanied by attendants waited outside on wooden benches and in wheelchairs holding their belongings in their laps. They were the lucky ones going home with loving friends and family. Angela wondered if her mother would ever be so fortunate.

A familiar voice greeted her, making her turn around. "Hello, Cookie, I'm sorry about your mother. I came because I felt somehow you needed me."

It was Carl!

It had only been a few days since she had left him in Valdosta but it seemed like an eternity. She went right into his arms. "Oh, Carl, I'm so glad you're here. My mama's not doing well. What am I going to do? This all happened because of me. Oh God, I'm so glad you're here. You gotta help us." She held onto him for dear life and let all her tears go. They sat down on the sofa. He never let her go.

Pearce stood out of sight in the hallway, angry because this time he was a witness to his woman showing affection to another man. He wanted to be the one to comfort her. It took everything he had not to push open that mahogany door but he wasn't ready to go to jail yet. He would talk to Angela when he could. Now he was going to Rose's room to tell her he was sorry for taking her only child away to Georgia and for her not to give up. He loved Rose even though some people said he didn't like her. He just wanted Angela to listen to him more and stop doubting him. Of course he loved Rose because she was always there for him and Angela. She could have turned him in herself but she really stuck by him and Angela. And it had been his crime, not hers. He couldn't go to his brother's funeral because his mother told him she would be okay and that she couldn't take it if the police were to catch up with him while he was paying respects to his dead twin brother, Paul.

That was the only time Pearce was willing to take a chance on being caught. He had regretted the decision he made to run away from the law in Los Angeles and he really wanted to go back. He longed to hold and comfort his mother and the rest of his family but he couldn't stand the thought of being behind ugly prison walls He knew he wouldn't like holding no cold iron bars looking down no hot stinking hallway wishing every minute to be free.

He walked on down the hall to the Intensive Care Unit muttering, "Okay, anybody who wants to get me come on. I'm taking my chances now going to see my mother-in-law and that's it."

When Pearce heard the news in Georgia, he couldn't believe it. Not Rose in the hospital. Critical? She smoked a lot and he smoked a lot too. He made a mental note to himself to quit. Now he decided to go see Angela. He figured she would surely need him by now and this would be the perfect time to patch things up with her. A time when she needed so much support.

Pearce talked to Rose but she only made gestures and smiled at him. She pointed to her tube and made a motion for him to take it out. Her eyes pleaded with him and she started to whimper. He rubbed her hands gently with his and left the room without anyone noticing him. He went down the hall to the solarium and wondered how long it would take before Angela found out he was in Los Angeles. He figured Rose had told her that he had called her. He sat in a big chair looking out the window facing the green and brown hillsides and slopes and curves on Crenshaw Boulevard, thinking about his whole family, his mother, father, sister, brother, his deceased brother and his little girl. And now he just did something foolish again.

He wondered if he did the right thing. *Damn, will I ever do anything right?* Then he lost it and started to cry, holding a soft handkerchief over his face.

He lay back on the recliner and closed his eyes with the handkerchief still on his face. Someone touched his shoulder and he looked around quickly. It was Angela. "Pearce, you really did come. To turn yourself in? The nurses told me that someone was here." Then Angela stood there, her face expressionless. "She's gone." She sank down on the floor as if all the energy had drained from her with only the thick carpet to cushion her body which was still in shock.

"Angela," he said. "It was my fault. I know she was worried about you and Candi. That's why I came on out here. I know how hard this is on you, Angela, and I'm sorry about everything I did to you. I can make it up to you and Candi. Come over here. Sit by me."

"No, I'm really okay," she said and sat down on the other chair across from him. "Candi wanted to see her grandmother so much."

This time Carl stood in the doorway watching and he didn't want to believe what he was seeing. Angela looked around, saw Carl, got up and walked quickly toward him. Pearce got up too and said, "If it ain't Carl Finch here to help out my wife." Everybody was silent.

Carl said, "If only we could make it all okay. This is a very sad time."

Pearce said, "It's her mother. My mother-in-law, my baby's grandmother. I'm going on to visit Candi." He looked at Angela and continued softly, "You said she's at Rose's sister's house. Mazie, right?"

Angela stood there and looked at him not really wanting him to go even though he had treated her so bad. Somehow, it was like he was her mother leaving her all over again.

"Yeah, she's there now. We'll be there soon." She looked at Carl.

Pearce turned to Carl again. "I'm going to see my little sweet girl and I'll take care of her for a little while. I'm sure she's gonna be happy to see me. Don't you all worry about me because I'm gonna be just fine." Then Pearce kissed Angela briefly on the lips. "See you soon, Mrs. Jones. Oh excuse me. I'm sorry. I forgot for a minute. I thought you was still my wife. Silly me." He stood there and looked at Angela for a brief moment then walked away.

Angela and Carl just stood there not too close to one another yet. They thought they somewhat had Pearce's blessings but they didn't want to push it with him. They sat on the sofa and she rested her head on his chest. Carl took a deep breath and finally spoke. "Cookie, tell me what you need. I know things are crazy right now but know that I am always here for you and I'll see that everything is taken care of for you. Don't worry." He rubbed her soft black hair which smelled like mango and coconut oils.

They both looked around quickly. Pearce came into the room again looking as though he forgot something. "Excuse me," he said. "I don't think I like this shit. Your momma just passed away and you up in here cheating. I don't believe I'm looking at this. I bet you all just want me to turn myself in and rot in jail."

Carl spoke again. "This is a hospital and let's remember we are all under a lot of stress."

Angela took Pearce by the hand and led him into the hallway. "Let's be real about this. What about our daughter? We have to build a life for her and we have to start now." She became angry and stared at him. She said, "My mother would not like this."

A police officer approached them slowly and confronted Pearce.

"Got some questions for you, sir, would you come this way please." The officer tried to lead him away and Pearce turned and looked at Angela. "Was this your way of getting me out of your life? I thought you and I meant more than that to each other."

Carl came out in the hallway.

"Oh, you called them," Pearce said, "'cause you wanted my wife and daughter."

Carl said, "What is he talking about? Called them for what?" He looked at the policeman. "I'm an attorney and I want to know what the problem is. My name is Carl Finch and this is Angela Jones."

The officer spoke quietly considering the fact he was in a hospital unit. "With all due respect, sir, it's none of your business right now but we are investigating a possible…." He stopped talking. Then he went on. "Just routine questioning in a case like this. We have reason to believe there may have been foul play in the death of Mrs. Adams. And after checking out some of the visitors, we determined that Los Angeles County has been looking for this man here, Pearce Jones, for some time. Just some routine questions, sir, but we gotta take him downtown. Oh, Mr. Finch, stick around huh? That would be a good idea. And another thing, it's real nice of you to be here for Miss Jones." He looked at Angela. "I'm really sorry about your mother. This your husband? I thought so. See you all soon." Then he left with Pearce looking back at them with an unnerving stare.

Angela's heart pounded. She was scared. Pearce really was going to jail. Now he would be forced to deal with being a fugitive, even though he thought she turned him in. After they took Pearce, Angela and Carl stayed in the room sitting on the couch quietly. Ten minutes later the officer came back and said the two of them were also under suspicion for murder and all the visitors in Rose's room were suspects.

"That can't be true. We don't know anything about anything. That's crazy. Didn't she pass on naturally? We were in there with her and everything was done for her that should have been done. This is way too much for Angela. Give us a break please, we are trying to mourn here."

The officer looked at Carl and then at Angela. "Either I take you both in or one of you better start talking. "

They looked at each other.

The officer spoke again and reached into his jacket pocket. "First question. Tell me about this note. We have concrete evidence that it was in your possession, Mrs. Jones. Didn't know you left it in the chapel?"

The note said, All things work together for the good for those called according to his purpose. Consider it done.

Chapter 8

TOM ADAMS CALLED MAZIE'S HOUSE to see if Angela and his granddaughter, Candi, had arrived yet.

Mazie, in shock over losing her baby sister, took a deep breath. "Tom, where have you been all these years? Honey, it's too late. She is gone. Rose is gone. She got sick and she couldn't snap out of it. A better place she is in, hon."

"Oh my gosh. Wait a minute. Damn. That can't be true, Mazie. Where's Angela now? I mean when—I mean what could have happened to my wife? I was on my way back to straighten out some property issues. Where's my daughter?"

Mazie answered in a real soft tone, "They up there at the hospital. I got the baby right here with me. I don't think she knows her grandma is gone. Her daddy, Pearce, gone be here in a minute to see her. That Pearce was sometimes a sore spot with Rose. She always said she wished she could understand him and Angela. That situation was a mess. I know it worried her. Lord, now she's gone. Oh God, poor Angela. To come back and find this going on," she sobbed.

Tom's voice broke through snapping her out of the crying spell. "Mazie, I'm coming out there right now. Just one more thing. What situation you talking about with Pearce and Angela? They were living somewhere in Georgia lately. Right?"

"Well, I guess you might as well know, Tom. Pearce was involved in that big robbery on Wilshire some years back and he left the state. You know. Jumped bail. His family helped him leave. Then Angela followed him down there. That's how they got in Georgia. She finally left him and come back to this."

"What? Hold on, Mazie. Are you telling me that dude had my baby girl running from the law? I know he better stay right wherever he is, 'cause he don't want to run into me. I'm almost there. Gotta go see my baby girl now before something else goes wrong. Mazie, you can tell my baby girl I'm coming to straighten things out."

"They still at the hospital. I don't know what's taking them so long. Some friend of hers is there with her too named Carl from Valdosta and she say they coming here soon. I would go but I got Candi here with me."

He let out a big moan. "Oh my, my, my. No problem, Mazie. Stay put. I'm close to the hospital." *Click.* He hung up.

Mazie wondered why he came back after so long. Did he think Angela would be glad to see him after living most of her life not even hearing from him? She looked around the huge living room. The walls were light olive green. Wallpapered with bright yellow and dark green borders. Candi sat at her little desk with the chalkboard that Rose had purchased for her, the chalk in her fist drawing little circles over and over. Mazie didn't know what to say to her. Candi did really well with Mazie even though she had never been around her. Her sister Rose had let her talk to Candi on the telephone sometimes when Candi and Angela were living in Valdosta. Mazie watched Candi draw the circles over and over with a blank stare on her face. Every now and then she would turn her chubby little face toward Mazie and give her a smile. Mazie got up from the cherrywood dining table, walked over to Candi and said, "Honey, how about we look at some really cool pictures. Would you like that?"

Candi nodded her head. "Okay, can I see my daddy?"

"Sure, honey. Let's see what we can find. Must be some pictures of your mom and dad in here somewhere. What you think?" Mazie walked over to the sofa and sat down. Candi followed her lead and climbed up beside her as Mazie opened a dark brown leather photo album. The first picture they saw was Rose and Angela in the park and Rose was pushing Angela on the swing. Angela was about four years old with some shiny black patent leather shoes on. Her thick braids were pinned up across her head. Mazie pointed to Rose. "That's your grandmother." Then she touched Angela's image. "That's your momma when she was your size." Candi sucked her thumb and leaned her head on Mazie's left arm. "When is Mommie coming back? I want my mommie!"

Mazie kept turning the pages slowly. "Your mommie will be here soon. Oh, here's another picture of your grannie, her husband, Tom, which is your grandfather, your momma and some little boy. He's looking down so we can't see his face. I don't know who he is."

Candi took her thumb out of her mouth and placed it on the little boy in the picture. She raised her voice a little as though she saw a surprise. "That's my daddy!"

Mazie folded her hands in her skinny lap and gave Candi a sideways look, then she looked back at the photo, and thought to herself, "Oh my. This must be that picture. I thought Rose had got rid of this one. Lord, please don't let that secret come out now."

Chapter 9

THE POLICE OFFICER CAME BACK and told Angela and Carl they were under suspicion and they would be hearing from him if he needed anything more. After he left them with his business card, Angela said to Carl, "This is crazy. Why would they suspect somebody of doing that to her, I hated to see her like that but"—Carl stepped back a little and put his hand under her chin and tilted her face up so he could look down into her eyes. "Angela, do you need to tell me something?"

She held her head down again, looked away and started crying. "I don't know what happened in that room. I couldn't take seeing her like that anymore."

He continued standing there close to her not touching her at all now.

"Okay," she said. "I told you that I wanted to but I didn't have the nerve."

"Cookie, you know I want to marry you someday. I know this is not the time but I just want you to know that I want to spend the rest of my life with you but for now we are going to work on everything together."

A tall heavy-around-the-middle man walked into the waiting room with his hands in the air. "I don't think anybody should be getting married without me. I want to give away my own beautiful daughter this time."

Angela looked at him wide-eyed, speechless. Carl remained silent.

Tom held his hand out to Carl. "I'm Tom Adams. Angela's long-lost father."

Angela didn't know what to think or what to say. She remained silent. Carl spoke for her and himself. "I'm sure I'm pleased to meet you, sir." He put his arm around Angela's shoulder. "Cookie. This man is saying he is your father. You should say something to him. How about hello?"

She answered, "Okay, I'm glad you came back to your family. Welcome back, daddy dear," she said sarcastically. She folded her arms across her chest and moved closer to Carl.

Her daddy answered, "We got to start somewhere. Come here. It hasn't been that long since I saw you. Honey, you know I came back because I missed you." He hugged her gently and she relaxed and even felt safe again in his arms like she remembered when she was just a kid. He smelled fresh and clean like he had just showered and she could smell his minty cologne.

They all sat down on the big sofa, Angela in the middle. They sat in silence for a few seconds looking at the small television on the oak table in the corner. The Lakers were at the Great Western Forum playing the Suns. It was the third quarter and the Lakers were ahead by three points and thousands of fans were making as much noise as they could. Nothing seemed to erase the pain that Angela was feeling right now.

Her father spoke again. "Do you love this man here asking for your hand? And is he good for you? That Pearce wasn't no good and maybe I was a little no good myself sometimes. I'm sorry 'bout your momma. And I'm even sorrier that I didn't spend more time with you. But I want you to believe one thing and that is I loved you and her very much but we didn't stay together because we just didn't know enough about life. Your daddy's here now for you and Candi. "

Carl interrupted, "The funeral arrangements are being made by my office. I'm waiting for your answer, Cookie. From the way things are going now we better hurry up and plan a wedding. The police are saying that somebody might have disconnected the machine. What a world. What a world. I want us to have something exciting to look forward to once all this is over."

Tom said, "Yeah, you might be right about that, Carl. That's why God gave us the rainbow. So we could have hope after the storm. And that's good of you to make funeral arrangements for my wife. That should be up to me now. What you think about that, Angela?"

"Daddy, you were not here to help me and Mazie. Let's just do what we can."

Carl spoke. "I'm only doing what I thought was best. Trying to help Angela. And I want to marry her. Do you have a problem with her marrying a white man? Please don't answer that yet. Just know I will take care of her."

Angela said, "Well, Carl, I can see myself married to you. Maybe it will be the rainbow I need."

Carl took her hands in his. "Where do you want to go, my love, for our wedding? Italy? Africa, Mazatlan, South of France? My family has resorts in the Caribbean. We can use the penthouse for the guests. I'll have my secretary, Praline, make the travel arrangements for us and your father, Candi, your aunt Mazie." He looked at Tom. "Your guest, sir? Of course you will bring your lady friend."

Tom shook his head. "I don't know about going no long way and bringing no lady friend. But I know what you are doing now. You trying to stop my baby from hurting so much by giving her something to celebrate. All in good time, and I usually travel by myself."

Angela shook her head.

He held her by the shoulders. "You think I could at least do that for you since you my only girl? I know what you are thinking. You are a lot like your momma was, but I'm not going into that right now. Okay! I'm going and I'll find me a nice companion to take. Don't you all worry about ol' Dad. But first, I think we need to bury your momma." He sat back down on the little love seat and wiped tears from his eyes.

* * *

Sergeant Eddie Best stretched out on the sands of Rosarita Beach after he applied some almond-scented sunscreen to his rosy cheeks. Today was his day off and he thought the big frosty white waves would get his mind off his stressful workload down at headquarters. But lying here on the lukewarm white sand only made it easier to think about his recent case. He kept asking himself, "Who could have pulled the plug on poor Mrs. Adams?" He had some good suspects in mind and he knew in hospital cases like this it was hardly ever the first one you thought it was. He'd been on the forensics team for eight years. He was thirty-five then, newly married and he hated some things his wife did too sometimes. Like when she got on him for being a little late even though she said she would understand that issue before they tied the knot. Husbands are always the first suspects even though this time, poor Mrs. Adams was the ex. It was not uncommon for exes to get the ax either, and this case was going to take some unraveling.

He didn't really think Pearce did it but he had to hold him because Los Angeles wanted him for a prior case. And he talked about how much he loved Angela and came to Los Angeles to help her out in this time of need. And Sergeant Eddie didn't figure that killing your mother-in-law was a way to get your ex back. Or was it? Yeah, Pearce talked a lot about Angela, but still denied having anything to do with the robbery on Wilshire five years ago. Why would a wanted criminal show up in a hospital in the city that he was wanted in, where all kinds of people were?

Just then he noticed someone familiar jogging along the water's edge. Dr. Henry? He said to himself, "A likely candidate," and chuckled. Why would ol' doc want to do something like that? Sergeant Eddie always posed the question about his cases to himself in the form of a statement that he would have to finish such as, "Dr. Henry would commit this crime on Mrs. Adams because…" In this situation the answer was because he was being paid off! Everyone has a price but who would pay? And besides, the Hippocratic oath specifically states that medical people are to preserve life above all. Above all? Above all the heart is deceitful and desperately wicked. Okay Eddie, he said to himself again, you are way off key here. He turned over and just not to be a fool, he wrote the doc's name on his notepad. Alex Henry, MD.

Sergeant Eddie looked at his black leather banded Timex watch. "Oh shit! It's my wedding anniversary and it's almost six o'clock and I told Lulu I would be home by seven." Well luckily he had her gift already because he learned over the last eight years to have the gift ahead of time just in case he was ever running late. He gathered his belongings, practically shoved them in his backpack and grabbed his lounge chair and his small ice chest. He made a quick stop by his favorite florist who always had ready bouquets of red roses for any occasion. He had known Charlie and Judy so long that all he had to do was stop briefly outside on the curb and go inside. No matter what they were doing they always stopped and handed him an arrangement so he could go on his way quickly. They knew he would come by later and settle up the debt and tell them how the big evening went.

He made it home by seven-thirty and went in through the kitchen entrance. Lulu had red and white candles glowing everywhere. The small duplex smelled like fresh roses mixed with vanilla. Everything smelled good. The roast beef and red potatoes and asparagus were covered up on the stove. A two-tiered chocolate cake sat in the middle of the oval dining table. It was trimmed in red with little red and pink roses on top. Eight minia-ture red candles were perched on it ready to be lit. All was quiet with no signs of Lulu. He stopped in his tracks and sang out, "Where is my gorgeous wife? The love of my life." He slowly walked into the living room and saw her sitting on the camel colored love seat in silence with her eyes glued to the TV news channel. She looked beautiful sitting there in a red silk robe with red garters and black stockings and straight black hair covering her shoulders.

He said, "Honey, turn around and take the flowers. You are so beautiful."

She jumped up and took the flowers, walked into the dining room and set them on the table. "Eddie! How many times have I told you I worry about you? Eddie," she whined. "What does it take? Honey, I get scared."

He stood behind her very close and rubbed her bare shoulders very lightly with his hands.

She turned around and held him close. "Eddie, I don't want you late anymore. Okay?"

He took the champagne bottle and filled the frosty cold goblets with the golden sparkling liquid, handed her one and made a toast. "To my sexy baby doll. What are you going to feed me?" She reached for the strawberries and cream. "I thought we would start with dessert first." She took a handful and fed him slowly. He licked her hands and fingers one at a time. She moaned. His hand gently brushed her breasts and felt her hard nipples through the silky fabric. She kissed him while she unbuttoned his shirt and then led him to the bedroom.

Chapter 10

LATER THAT NIGHT, SERGEANT EDDIE WOKE UP and looked at the clock on the nightstand. A red number three with two dots and two zeroes stared back at him. He looked over at Lulu. He stroked her soft shiny hair quietly, not wanting to wake her up. The streetlight came in the window through the lavender curtains. It was springtime in Los Angeles and you could smell the white magnolias and purple jasmine through the screened window.

Lulu sat up abruptly and grabbed a glass of ice water that she had left there earlier. It was still cool. She took a big gulp, kissed Eddie on the back of the neck and let the cool water run down his back.

He moved out the way. "What was that for? I tried not to wake you. You are too touchy, bean pole. Can't a man touch a broad's hair a little bit at night?"

She reached over and turned on the small lamp on her nightstand and sat up. "Now what's bothering you? Come on, tell me, Eddie. I'm not losing all this sleep for nothing. Start talking."

"That poor Mrs. Adams. Somebody for sure pulled that plug. Her daughter had gone away a while ago with that fugitive. She wouldn't come back to do away with her mother. There was no insurance money left anywhere. And whoever did it had the nerve to pull the plug out from the wall."

Lulu said, "Honey, this could very well be a sympathy thing. Someone could have done it to give her a break from suffering. Who would hate to see her suffer the most? Her sister, Mazie, could have done it. Maybe Pearce felt vindictive 'cause his wife went home to her. Who knows what evil lies in the hearts of men. Many, many men."

Eddie said to her, "Okay, smarty-pants, what makes you think it had to be a man?"

She sat up real nice and cute and stared him in the face, and said in that soft voice, "Because men are real stupid, Eddie. No woman would be dumb enough to do that. If it was a woman she would probably get someone else to do it, 'cause women can get men to do anything and women just ain't that stupid."

"Here we go again, Lulu. Damn it! You make me want to start smoking again. You always want to help me solve something but you start talking that stupid men stuff. Okay, lady. If it was a stupid man—and I'm not saying it was—what stupid idiot trifling man did that to poor Mrs. Adams?"

She looked at him for a moment and said, " Hey, those detective magazines of yours give me a lot of ideas, but I'm not ready to guess yet, Eddie. It's coming to me. You wait and see. You know I like to think about these things." She massaged his shoulders and held him in her arms and lay down with him. She kissed his forehead and rubbed his red hair till he went back to sleep.

Chapter 11

CARL ANGELA AND TOM JOINED HANDS in the hospital waiting room and kneeled down in a circle like they used to do when Tom was with Rose and Angela was just a baby. Tom said a prayer. "Lord let us find peace in this situation and keep your arms around us as we come back to this good-for-nothing city of Los Angeles. Forgive me for my sins and for leaving my wife and children. Take care of everyone in this family and all our friends. Lord, if anyone did any harm to my Rosie, please bring them to the front line so we can deal with them accordingly—or you, Lord. You, Lord, deal with them, for it is not for us to bring justice to our fellow man. Lord, only you know how to deal with this. And Lord, let me get along with everybody this time. Amen."

Angela sat down again and faced her father. "Daddy, you have to tell me what that picture was all about. This is as good a time as any. Who was that little boy?"

"Honey, I promise as soon as we get over to Mazie's I'll tell you. I hope you can wait till then. Daddy's all worn out right now. Let's just get over to Mazie's. We have done all that we can do here. I'm really sorry about what happened to Pearce but I sure hope he didn't do anything to Rosie. He should have quit running long ago but I know he didn't mess with that machine." He paused and looked at Angela and then at Carl and shook his head from side to side and let out a deep sigh. "Looks like we all got a lot of explaining to do. Can't wait to see my grandbaby and I bet she got a lot to say if she anything like her grandmother. That's if she will talk to me because she don't even know me."

He looked at Angela, standing there holding Carl's hand. "I know I got a lot of catching up to do but everything is going to be fine now. Don't you worry. That's what daddies are for. To make everything better. Wait and see. You don't say much baby girl, but I betcha that little Candi just like her grandmother. Love to talk and tell folks what to do."

Carl stated, "I guess she really is like her grandmother. She never had a problem telling me and Angela what to do." He laughed.

"That's right, Daddy. I know she's gonna love you but you have to stay around and get to know her. You know with all the stuff that's been happening with Pearce...What were you going to tell me about the picture you sent me on the train?"

"Oh, that picture tells a thousand stories. Baby girl, when we get there, I'll tell you everything from A to Z. Promise. Let's go." He looked at Angela with impatience. "What? She's ten minutes away. Daddy don't like to tell on people. You will see for yourself soon." They went on out the doors to the hallway and out of the building.

* * *

She had been watching them while they prayed. She wanted to shout out. "I know what happened to Mrs. Adams. I didn't mean for it to be like that." She slipped her hands in her jacket pockets and went on down the hall stopping briefly at the nurse's station. Then she went out of the side door and down to the parking lot to her silver and red Mercury Cougar.

Chapter 12

PEARCE WAS THANKFUL THAT SOME YEARS AGO he had found a book about remembering names and numbers. Once he had decided to leave California to avoid prosecution he read it from cover to cover. He had tested it very well with the phone numbers and addresses of his family and friends. The book showed a person how to associate crazy situations with names and people and numbers. He figured there was no point in carrying this information everywhere he went. Plus since the cops were looking for him he might have to get up and run any minute with just the clothes on his back and the few emergency fund dollars he always kept in his pockets.

This time he relied on his skills to remember the contact information of the only man who had the money to help him without a doubt. He picked up the hard cold black phone receiver and wiped the moisture off with his rough shirt. He called Hop Sing in San Diego.

"Hey man. They got me in this jail for some crap I didn't have anything to do with. I told them years ago I wasn't guilty and it was somebody who looked like me. They say I got to get an attorney and then they had the nerve to question me about some plug that was tampered with at the hospital. Angela's mom died and they say it's foul play. What that got to do with me, I don't know. Angela and that man of hers don't even want to talk to me. Can you help me get out of here? I'll pay you back."

"Pearce. I told you stay in Georgia. You have trouble for L.A. You suppose to be taking care of the Inn. Who did you leave in charge? Not Diamond, I hope. There is always problem with Diamond and her friends. Jamie, Stella, Mike. I go back Valdosta now. Oh no, Pearce. You in trouble. Hop Sing don't help you now. You come back Georgia. Maybe work for me when you free. Hop Sing see you later. You write Hop Sing letter. No more call collect from jail. Hop Sing go Georgia now and take care Inn. Hop Sing hang up now. Oh Pearce, don't drink the water! Ha ha." Click.

Damn, how do I keep getting myself into these things? Pearce hung up the jail phone and quickly got out of the way so another inmate could take his turn. He strolled slowly down the corridor with his hands in the pockets of his oversized orange jumpsuit. It felt rough on his warm sweaty body. The harsh detergent they used to wash the clothes in here irritated him just like his dislike for being locked up and he knew he would be free soon. One way or another. Coming to see Rose was not a good idea even though he wanted to see Angela. Anyway, he had not planned on coming so soon. It was just that Rose needed to know how sorry he really felt and he wanted to help her. At least he had helped her and that was the one good thing that came out of him coming back to Los Angeles. He couldn't tell anybody about Rose because no one would understand. No one ever did understand him. Now he had to keep this to himself forever. Yes, only she knew what happened. Who cared now, anyway? He was locked up. Probably never get free again. But he couldn't let Carl have Angela. He would find a way out and he would make everything okay when he was free again.

He lay on his narrow bunk and looked up at the dingy white ceiling and wished he was back in Valdosta at Nash's fishing hole and lying on the quiet waterfront staring up at the dark night and the faraway stars. He wondered how long he would have to wait to lay down by the lake and stare up at the bright stars again.

* * *

She drove to her apartment on Wilshire. She knew Pearce was in jail now so she decided to write him a letter and let him know that she had his back and not to worry. She would not let him take the rap for Rosie and she would let him know she was going to tell the truth before too long. She removed her brown leather gloves and wiped them off with a linen dish towel. It was a habit of hers to wipe off the gloves, but she thought, who would find them or her for that matter. She thought she worried for nothing. She placed the bowl of cat tuna on the floor beside the coffee table and gently smoothed her cat's sandy-colored fur while she watched her eat.

Her feet were tired and she removed her red leather boots, put her feet up on the ottoman and quickly fell asleep right there on the sofa. She had barely closed her eyes when the phone rang. She answered it quickly. All she heard was a voice on the other end saying it was a collect call from the jail. It was Pearce. She got scared right then and decided not to talk to him now because she still had a lot of thinking to do and she was exhausted. She hung up the phone and said, "I'm sorry, sweetcakes. I just can't talk to you yet." Then she pulled the phone cord out of the wall. She went to the huge master bedroom and looked in the mirror at her reflection.

She smiled at herself. She was beautiful. And every man wanted her. Her soft hair was black and fuzzy but long and shiny. Her eyes were light brown. Her flawless skin was the color of golden honey. Her breasts were above average size for her five foot seven frame. "I've got to get out of here." She threw some clothes and all her personal things in the suitcases. Pearce was going to keep calling and if she didn't talk to him he was going to tell the police about her. She knew he couldn't be trusted and now he was probably going to blackmail her. How come of all people he was the one to see her come into the hospital? The best thing she could do now was go back to Valdosta and let them solve this shit on their own. She looked in the mirror again. "Without yours truly, Miss Bitch."

Chapter 13

AT EIGHT P.M., CARL, ANGELA AND TOM rang the doorbell at Mazie's place, waking up her and Candi. Candi ran ahead of Mazie and reached for the doorknob. "Mommie, Mommie. Mommie's at the door."

Mazie sighed as she walked quickly to the door. "Oh God, lord, lord, lord, lord, don't let it be no mess today while we getting ready to bury my sister," she said as she gently moved Candi out of the way. "Honey, always see who it is before you open the door. Let auntie look out the keyhole." She looked and she could see Tom, Angela's dad, with an impatient look on his face. Finally he said, "I know you hiding from me, Mazie. Open this door, woman. Let me see my granddaughter. Candi," he yelled, "you in there? Tell your auntie"—before he could finish, the door flew wide open. Candi ran to Angela and Carl. Tom hugged Mazie and then tried to hug Candi. She held onto Angela for dear life and turned her head away. Tom said, "It's okay. She's a good little girl and she shouldn't be talking to strange people." After Mazie met Carl in person, they sat down. Angela looked at Tom without saying a word.

Tom began. "Okay, Mazie. I know this is hard for you. And it sure isn't the best of times with what done happened to Rosie and her being your sister and all but it's time to get all this out in the open."

"Okay," she sighed. "You tell it 'cause you know what happened better than me."

Carl interrupted. "Excuse me, but do you want me to leave the room?"

Angela looked at Tom. Tom looked at Mazie. Mazie spoke.

"Angela, go lay the baby down since she's falling asleep. She don't need to hear this. "

Angela returned quickly and Rose had the picture book out turning the pages. They all sat close so they could see the photos. Tom said, "Here is the picture you saw already, Angela. That's me, your momma, and you as a little runt. That little boy is your momma's other son. One of them. They were twins. The other boy was with their real daddy, when this picture was taken."

Angela looked at him. "Real daddy? What? How did that happen? No. No. No. I can't take this. I just can't take this. That's it!"

She started to get up but Carl took her hand again and said softly, "Sit down, Angela. You wanted to know and now is the best time to find out. Pretty soon we will all be fine. Relax. We're all here to work this out."

Tom breathed a deep sigh and looked at his daughter. When he saw that she had calmed down he went on, "We lost track of them. You were just a little girl. We all did our best. Even Mazie helped Rose with them. They all did the visiting back and forth and finally Rosie's heart was broken because she decided to let them go stay with their father. She did it for you and me, Angela, but by then our marriage was too far gone to mend it."

Angela remained silent and Tom went on, "This was all while we were married. Bottom line, she fooled around on me. Yep, women do it too. But, that's why she always loved you so much, baby. You were all we had and she couldn't have any more children. That was the main reason we split up. It was just a mess, so I stayed away so long. I really missed you Angela. That's why I came back to see you and to let you know what really happened. I know you may not understand and you might be still mad at me but at least you know what happened, for whatever it is worth. I'm sorry it all came out at this time and since it did I think we all need each other now more than ever."

Angela looked at her dad, then Carl and back at her dad. "What are their names? If they are my brothers I should know their names. Since nobody cared enough to tell me about my own brothers! I can't believe my own mother would keep something like that from me. If there is anything else I need to know, it can wait. Pretty soon somebody's gonna say that I'm not even my mother's." She laughed. "I wouldn't be surprised!"

Mazie sighed. "Honey, I know this is a lot for you but she never wanted to hurt you. That's why she didn't try to stop you from leaving California to go to Georgia with Pearce. She thought you all might keep your family together. We all figured there was a small chance that it would work but still in all it was a chance. A small chance is better than nothing at all. And here you are back in Los Angeles." Mazie started to cry. Angela sat beside her and hugged her. "Oh, Auntie. It's all going to be fine. I know you miss your baby sister. We are all here now and we are going to go forward and make everything work out. Don't worry now."

Carl asked, "So where are Angela's brothers?"

Mazie answered, "Their names are Joseph Jr. and John. They're about twenty years old now. I really think they were seeing Rose every now and then. She didn't tell me everything even though we always been real close. Said she was going to clear all this up with you, Angela, when you got here from Georgia this time. So many questions unanswered."

Tom spoke. "You know I told you all that junk when you called me from the train station because I didn't want you to think bad of your mother until I could see you and tell you the truth. But that picture was the real clue. I figured I would get your attention that way so you would at least let me tell you the truth."

Mazie looked at Tom. "I know you don't want to talk about this but Joseph, the boys' father, came back around trying to get with Rose but he was married at the time and had fooled her real good already. It was a mess. It was. It really was."

Angela laid her head on Carl's shoulder. "I can't take any more news. I'm going to leave that one alone now and get ready to lay my mother to rest."

"Sure, pumpkin," Tom answered. "I'm so sorry about everything. But everything always works out for the best." He stood up. "I'll be going on my way now, I'll see you all this weekend at the services. Saturday morning, right? Eleven o'clock." He walked to the door and looked back at Mazie. "We can get through this. We both loved Rosie, so we gotta take care of what she left behind. I believe those boys are somewhere close and we are making progress. I just about accomplished everything I came to do. And I do mean everything. It's amazing what evil lies in the hearts of men and of course women. I'm out!" The door shut behind him.

Angela said, "I love my daddy but he has always been a big fucking liar. Tomorrow we'll sort this out some more."

She looked at Mazie. Mazie threw her hands up. "Hey, as far as I'm concerned, all that stuff he said can be taken with a grain of salt. Now tell me what happened with Pearce. Why do they have that boy in jail?"

Chapter 14

SERGEANT EDDIE WALKED SLOWLY INTO HIS OFFICE at the precinct and sat at his mahogany desk. He took the silver cufflinks out of his white shirt and pushed the sleeves up all the way to his elbows. Then he loosened his tie. "Let me do some real thinking now. It's about time to get some action on some of these lovely suspects. Yes, lovely indeed." He pushed all the extra clutter out of the way making some room in the middle for his sketch notepad. He liked drawing people and neighborhoods and putting faces on the suspects. So far there were Pearce, Angela, Carl, and Angela's dad Tom, who he just learned was in town. Of course the older sister, Mazie, and good ol' Doc Henry. He had taken note of the way Doc looked at Angela. Dr. Henry had given her a puzzled look when he saw her talking to Sergeant Eddie. It was as if he knew her personally. He would have to check into that further because he knew not to rule out anyone. Even those folks on the good side.

Looking back on his eight years in the law, he had never run into a case like this one. Poor Mrs. Adams was probably going to get better soon anyway or she wasn't and that would take her out of her misery anyway. So far, he had no concrete evidence on anybody. Whoever did it was just dumb enough to leave the plug out and smart enough to wipe the prints off. There were absolutely no prints on the cord or the plug which was rare for so many people had to check the machine daily to make sure it was working fine. The problem he saw with patients on life support in the ICU was that anyone could visit them and do whatever to them without cameras from the nurse's station picking anything up. The patients were tied down sometimes so they wouldn't pull out the plugs or the tubes. They couldn't use the call light and sometimes were intubated and unable to speak. He was all for monitoring visitors especially for the ones who were vulnerable. He didn't make the policies at the hospitals but he sure made some suggestions. Funny, he thought, they would guard a prisoner to keep anyone from harming him or keep him from getting away. The poor helpless patients like Mrs. Adams had no one to protect them unless their families had a restricted visitor policy in effect. This was going to be a very tough case, but there was no case too tough for the Los Angeles Homicide's best, Sergeant Eddie.

Everyone in the Intensive Care Unit was worried a little 'cause they couldn't believe someone would attempt something as horrendous as that in such a small place. Anyone could walk in any moment even if it was nighttime when there was very little traffic except the wide-awake nurses, some sleepy techs, respiratory treatment people and X-ray personnel. He decided he would go home, drink some brandy in front of his fireplace and think this all over while Lulu rubbed his shoulders with her firm soft fingers. Women seemed to make him feel smarter. There was something about that female species and the way they used their charms. They knew how to get what they wanted so they should be able to figure out everything else. But then there were some bimbos too.

Sergeant Eddie went down the stairs into the main lobby, put on his tan trench coat, and pushed open the heavy glass door against the blustery cold wind. Dried-up gold and red autumn leaves and dust blew everywhere including in his face. The usually crowded boulevard had just a few brave men and women rushing in and out of doorways to their nearby cars. The sky was a perfect light blue with a few white clouds scattered here and there. The sunshine was so bright but it was too cold to feel it.

What a beautiful clear day in L.A., he thought. *The winter air is so fresh and you can see the green mountains and dark hillsides against the gorgeous sky. If only this wind would stop I could get some leeway on this case. Maybe the answer is in the wind.* He continued on to his car, singing the lyrics of Stevie Wonder's version of "Blowin' in the Wind." "The answer my friend is blow- in' in the wind, the answer is blowin' in the wind."

Finally he reached the parking garage and removed a yellow flyer from his windshield and read it briefly. Some new camera shop on the boulevard. He tossed it on the ground. "Wow. I'd like to have a picture of that asshole who pulled the plug on poor Mrs. Adams." He put the Mercedes in gear and headed for his split-level home in Malibu. He stopped on the way and sat for an hour in the waterfront parking lot, looking at the boats and vessels on the Pacific. He rolled his window down, thankful that the wind had stopped, and took some deep breaths of the salty air. He went to the pay phone on the corner and checked in with his wife. "Hello Lulu honey, I'm on my way. You got dinner ready?"

She answered him and he could tell she smiled as she talked. "Yes, baby, and I got a new lavender silk dress just for you."

Eddie said, "New dress. Lavender? Silk? Sounds lovely, dear. Meet me under the lilac tree in the backyard so I can take it off."

That night Lulu sat in front of the crackling fireplace with Eddie's head in her lap.

"I'm sorry, my dear hubby," she said. "You know it had to be a woman, 'cause women are good at wiping stuff off and that would explain why the prints were all wiped off the plug and the cord."

"Wow! What a smarty-pants you are, dear wife. Did you learn that in one of those detective magazines too? Okay, how come she, if it was a she, didn't just shut it down with the switch? One touch. Bam! It's off!"

"Because, Eddie, I've worked in hospitals and I know about vents. When you turn it off by the switch, the readings stop right away and all the lights go off. It would start beeping before the person could leave the room. But when you pull the plug out it takes about two minutes before all the meters stop and the vent actually slows down to no air coming out of it. It's like a standby mode in case you are moving the patient or the machine quickly. She would have plenty of time to leave the room before anyone suspected anything."

Eddie rubbed her leg and kept listening.

She continued. "That's why it was left unplugged. Most of your suspects could leave quickly but remember most nurses on that unit stay in the room for more than two minutes. So they should have heard the beeping and realized something was wrong. Unless someone repeatedly plugged it and unplugged it giving the patient less and less air so eventually there was no air for survival."

Eddie stood up and faced her. "Am I to believe there were false readings from the machine after all that fiddling with it?"

"Sure," she said. "Reading all your detective magazines makes me kinda smart. Right? Anyway that's the reasoning I came up with. Eddie, you know sometimes I guess the right answers. Another thing about this case. If they had not left the plug out, no one would have known it was foul play. But obviously, the deed could not have been done any other way. Who the hell knows so much about vents? Gotta be a real smart bitchy person."

Chapter 15

SHE FELT AFRAID NOW OR MAYBE IT WAS EXCITEMENT as she looked on at the crowd gathering at the cemetery. No one seemed to notice her leaning on her red Cougar with her long legs stretched out with jet black stockings and a red suit that matched her car. She knew Pearce wasn't going to be there so no need to worry about getting noticed. How amazing to watch a situation she had something to do with even though she couldn't take all the credit.

Damn. What kind of power do I have? Well as long as Pearce is locked up and Angela is goo-goo eyed over that white man of hers, nobody should suspect me. Pearce saw me in the hospital and that's why he's calling to see if I know some shit. Well, hell no I don't know, so quit calling me.

I have my bags packed, plenty of gas, the money from the robbery that Pearce was framed for. He's a sucker if he thinks I'm going to tell the truth and set him free even though he would still be in trouble anyway. He might have told the old lady, Rose, what really happened with the robbery just to clear his conscience. I knew he couldn't keep his mouth shut too long. That's the reason I was so into doing her in.

She walked out a little ways onto the dirt and watched them. The heels of her black suede boots sank in the soft turf. She spotted a strange white man in a trench coat. *Aw shucks, he just might be a detective. Ha. Don't worry, Mr. Law, I'm out of here.* She got back in her car and drove off down the winding road a little too swiftly.

Sergeant Eddie turned around just in time to catch the tail end of a red Cougar going out of sight. He walked swiftly over to where the car had been parked, and looked at the footprints and the tire tracks from the car. "Hmm. Footprints can sometimes tell more than fingerprints." He glanced around the cemetery briefly to see if there was any more suspicious behavior going on. "I guess women do know how other women think and Lulu could have guessed right but time will tell." One thing about criminals, they always return to the crime scene in one way or another. Who was this tall ebony beauty with black fuzzy shoulder-length hair, looking like an afro? She didn't look familiar and he couldn't recall her face from any of the suspects he'd seen but she had curves to die for. Thank goodness the force had dusted the hospital room floor for prints, and man there were a lot.

Two days later they got a match on the tires and traced them back to Ms. Bitch's Cougar registered to Pearce Jones with a Chicago address of the Ritz-Carlton Hotel. Of course Pearce wasn't there now because he was in jail here in good old Los Angeles. That Pearce got around. He paid ten thousand cash for the red hot Cougar that was easy to trace because Mercury only made eighteen of those convertibles and only four of them were red. Sergeant Eddie figured Pearce should be eager to talk now. Any man who paid ten thousand cash for a car in Chicago, lived in Georgia and landed in jail back in L.A. shouldn't mind talking a little if it meant springing him early from the joint.

First he researched the phone logs from the county jail to see who Pearce had called. Some chick named Danielle in Georgia, someone called Hop Sing in San Diego and the last number that he called was owned by none other than Pearce Jones himself in a Los Angeles apartment. It was only in service for two weeks and the apartment had been occupied for two weeks as well. But for sure all the neighbors saw a tall black good-looking chick go in and out a few times mostly at night. The problem now was, where was she? And could he make Pearce talk?

Sergeant Eddie went to the jail and waited in the private legal room for Pearce to be brought out.

Pearce came out slowly not wanting to talk to anyone now especially no pig but he was thankful to get away from his crowded cell. He mumbled a greeting to the sergeant, sat at the table and asked for a cigarette right away, which Sergeant Eddie gave him and lit for him.

Sergeant Eddie watched Pearce slowly blow the smoke out and said, "You know what, Pearce? I sure saw a beautiful woman the other day sitting in a hot red Cougar. You know I got to thinking. What would a man have to do to have someone like her? I guess he could pay for her car. That is definitely an option. Hmm. What do you think, Pearce?"

Pearce slowly blew out four white smoke rings, then answered, "I suppose you want me to tell you who she is."

Sergeant Eddie lost his cool and raised his voice just a little. "Yes! Today would be a good fucking day to do it. Any time now!"

"Okay, man. I know who she is and I know what she got and I think I know what she did. She has been a pain in my neck since I left her in Chicago. Her and I really had something to do with the robbery back in 1971. She got most of the money, but she wanted me. That's why I went to Chicago from Valdosta to get my money from her and get a good lawyer and turn myself in. She wanted more than a robbery relationship. I admit, I played with it for awhile like any man would but I had to let her know that no woman on this earth was going to hold me captive. Not even the love of my life, my wife Angela. I left. She played games and said she didn't have the money no more. She said she spent some money on the car and blew the rest. The other fifty thousand was gone."

Eddie took the conversation back in a more relaxed tone. "Who is she and what is she doing here? You think she had it in for Mrs. Adams?"

"Hey," Pearce said, "I'm already locked up and I can't get no more locked up than I am. What's in it for me?"

"Time served."

"You mean to say, if I tell you who she is, I'm free? Free to leave this motherfucker?" Pearce couldn't believe this was not some kind of joke. "Man, what?"

Eddie stopped him. "As soon as we find her, you can go. This offer stands for the next ten minutes only. You have ten minutes between you and that locked door. I think one minute has passed already." He looked at the big black clock on the institution wall.

"Okay, I don't have a choice here. If you are a crooked cop and a liar then that will be my problem. Her name is Ms. B. That's all I ever knew."

"Ms. B. What's that stand for?"

"Ms. Bitch. That's what everyone I know called her. Don't worry. If I know her right, she be will downstairs trying to visit me soon. You see, Sergeant, I still got something she wants. I wasn't stupid enough to give her access to all the money. I told Angela's mother the whole story of the robbery and who was involved. She always told me that if I ever came clean with her she would stop being so hard on me and Angela and I felt guilty so I told her on her deathbed what happened. I was hoping she would live, though. But, and I repeat but, I didn't do anything to Rose and I don't know who did. I just felt sorry for her right then and there."

Sergeant Eddie continued, "And you risked your freedom."

"Hey man. I told you Ms. B. loved me. She scared and probably broke too. She was avoiding my calls then she realized her money was all gone. Now she's eager to talk to me. To answer your question about how to get a gorgeous woman like that. Easy. Just have more money than she got."

Eddie kept studying this man in wonderment. Pearce said, "Go hang out downstairs in the visiting area and see. You know what she looks like. Can't miss her long legs and dark fuzzy hair. A one-of-a-kind princess. Uh uh uh. Sweet but stings like a bee. Go get her. And if she did anything to Rose, I know nothing about it."

"Be back in an hour, Pearce. Don't go nowhere. Ha ha."

"Funny. Funny. Everybody got jokes."

Sergeant Eddie shook his head and walked on down the steps back to the jail lobby. When he got near the end of the stairway, he stopped in his tracks because right there through the front glass window he saw a familiar red car. The Cougar was parallel parking in the space right in front of the door. Sergeant Eddie's instincts told him to get out of the way. He slowly went back up the stairs backwards so he could see the bombshell suspect. This time her hair was straight and dark red and it reached her waistline. There was no mistaking her with that fine body and them sleek legs. She had on the same black leather boots that she wore at the cemetery.

Women like that made his job very hard. You could never tell if they were telling the truth or just being cute. Let her come inside and have the nerve to sign in to see Pearce. Obviously Pearce did know her well. Eddie watched her wait in the line behind three people. When she reached the counter, she pulled out her license. "I bet that doesn't say Miss Bitch on her ID," Eddie said to himself. "Okay, let her go in to see him." He went on up the stairs to the phone and called the front desk. "What's the name on that redhead's ID?"

Chapter 16

ANGELA AND CARL SAT ON MAZIE'S PATIO sipping hot lemon tea and listening to Donald Bryd's "Dominoes" coming from the house next door.

"Carl, is this ever gonna be all over? When will we be normal again? I know I've told you before but I have to tell you again how sorry I am. I love you so much for sticking by me in these trying times and I want to make it up to you. You'll see how much you mean to me when all this is over."

Carl sat next to her rubbing her shoulders gently. "Don't worry, honey. It will be okay as soon as we get married. Don't you worry at all. I got it all under control."

Angela kept thinking about her mother's services last week and trying to make some sense of it but nothing was going to make sense for a while. Probably never again. This situation was eating her insides and she cursed herself for not coming back to L.A. sooner. The piano music had played softy with the drums playing intermittently. Mellow and rhythmic. The small sanctuary was quiet except for an occasional whisper until Reverend Johnson started preaching. The choir was dressed in teal green robes with white trim.

Angela, Carl, Mazie and Tom had sat in the front pew at the St. James Baptist Church. Reverend Johnson preached a mighty powerful sermon that Saturday a.m. called "Are you ready for your maker?"

From the Book of Acts, Chapters 20–24: "None of these things shall move me. Are you sure you are ready to meet God? Let the church say amen. We all come into this world by the power of the Almighty with a free will. I want you all to think about yesterday for a minute. Not today! 'Cause this is a home-going service and Sister Adams is finally at rest. She has no more burden. She's been a good faithful servant. Look at your neighbor and say 'The burden is on you now.'" Everybody in the church repeated after him.

He continued while the organ player picked up the pace to match his rising and falling voice that went from a whisper to a shout. "The burden is on US! It's for us to carry on God's work. I'm talking about yesterday. Think about what you did yesterday. Were you nice to everybody yesterday? Some of you all were raising all kind of hell yesterday and smiling today. I'm talking about Friday! Not Saturday, but yesterday. Did you tell someone off? Did you cheat on your taxes? Did you look at that pretty lady down the street in the wrong way? You can't fool God today and go back to your ugly ways TOMORROW! The burden is on us to clean up our acts and spread the good news. Don't cry for Sister Adams. The best thing you can do for her is carry on the gospel, have a good life and spread the great news. Stop telling lies and spread the truth about Jesus. Let the church say amen!"

Angela had looked at her dad and thought to herself, "Please let him be lying about Momma and some other man. Please Lord, help me get through this and help me understand what happened to Momma. Please let the police find that the ventilator stopped working accidentally. Oh God." She had cried out, "Who would hurt my momma?" The ushers came to fan her and she felt weak with a burning in the middle of her stomach. She leaned against Carl and fell into a stupor. Like she was between sleep and awake. Her head spun and her heart was broken. She knew her mom's shell was in that yellow and brown coffin but her spirit was gone on to the Lord. But Angela kept seeing Rose's face in the hospital bed when she asked her to remove the tube and take her off the vent. Her mom had started to weep and Angela had rubbed her face and said, "No, no. It's going to be all right." Then her mom would stop crying. Angela knew then there had to be a better way.

The Reverend had stopped preaching and making people feel guilty. He stood quietly for a moment and motioned for the choir to stop singing. All of a sudden, he hummed the notes to "Amazing Grace." *How sweet the sound...* and the congregation hummed along with him.

Tom stood up suddenly and walked toward the back door. Angela watched him and on his way he saw Sergeant Eddie sitting in the back row. Tom paused when he got to the row he was in. They looked at each other briefly and Tom kept going. Sergeant Eddie waited until the door had closed and got up and walked down the aisle and right out the door behind him.

Angela replayed that scene over and over and she knew Carl really was worried now even though he wouldn't say it to her. She could tell. She decided to make him feel more relaxed and massaged his graying temples lightly with her soft fingers. Her fingers continued on down to his shoulders and his back. He lay down on the lounge chair face down and let her pamper him. She began kissing him and he hugged her close and unbuttoned her blouse exposing her breasts to the cool night air. He kissed her neck while he gently rubbed her. Just then, the patio door slid open. Mazie saw them and quickly closed the door going back inside. Angela jumped up, buttoned her blouse and opened the door. "What is it, Auntie? I'm sorry for what you saw..."

"Don't worry," she cut her off. "You have company in the den. Shall I ask him to come in?"

"Who is it now?" Angela asked with a puzzled look.

"Dr. Henry. Said he's been trying to get by here to see us and check on everybody. Are you up to it? I can tell him you're a little tired now."

"Yes, of course I'll see him, Auntie," Angela answered as she went through the door into the kitchen. "You know I always have time for our Dr. Henry because he has been so wonderful to us. Can you please give me and him some time alone? Just tell Carl I'll be out there soon."

Angela brushed her thick hair in place with her hands and straightened her green suede blouse as she walked slowly into the den. Dr. Henry remained sitting in the easy chair and smiled at Angela when she greeted him.

"What happened?" she asked. "Somebody said there was some foul play, Alex. I found the note later on. I didn't think anyone saw it but maybe they did. Everything is such a blur now but I think one of the officers at the hospital mentioned something about it."

Dr. Henry stood up and put both hands on Angela's shoulders, and said in a whisper, "Angela, look at me. What did you do? Tell me what you did. I was going to pull some strings to get the order to turn off the vent. I was not going to pull the plug myself. What did you do? I know you from way back and I know you can be stubborn as hell when you want your way. Damn it, Angela, you better tell me if you did it or not. You and I have helped each other our whole lives. This is no time for you to get stupid on me. This is some serious stuff here. Do you know what they call mercy killing?"

Angela looked up at him.

"Take a guess, my dear," he said.

She remained silent, giving him an almost evil look.

He said in a whisper, "Murder is what they call it."

Angela kept looking at him.

Dr. Henry shook his head and walked over to the soft love seat and sat down. "Talk to me! Did your boyfriend help you?" He raised his voice a little this time almost to his normal pitch. "Do I need to talk to him?" He looked around. "Where is he?"

Angela answered, "Okay. Okay. I understand what you are saying. And there is no reason to question Carl about any of this. Leave him out of this. I did not do it and if I did do it and tell you then you would know and that could hurt your career." She started to cry and touched his lips with her finger to silence him. Then she led him to the door and held it open. "Goodnight, doctor."

He took her warm hands and squeezed them gently in his before he left. "For some odd reason...maybe some evidence, a witness, or perhaps something else, they said it was some lady with heels on." He looked down at her boots and went out the door shaking his head.

Chapter 17

JOEY, THE DEPUTY CLERK AT THE JAIL LOBBY, spoke clearly over the black phone to Sergeant Eddie who was still waiting upstairs away from the saucer-eyed suspect. "Okay Sarge, I got it all right here. The ID is an Illinois driver's license with a Chicago address issued to a Connie Rogers. Thirty-five years old. Yes, that's the one who's here to visit Pearce Jones. Detain her? Okay, I guess we won't have any trouble holding onto her. We got her and she ain't going nowhere. Come on down to the interrogation room but take your time. She ain't too hard to look at. "

Sergeant Eddie came down the stairs, went to the door of the interrogation room, took a deep breath and hesitated a few seconds before entering. She was sitting there looking very calm like being in that room was no problem at all. When Sergeant Eddie walked in she perked up and smiled with a soft sexy voice, "Why hello, handsome. How are you?" Then her expression changed to a frown. "Oooooh. You're the policeman I saw at the funeral! Fancy meeting you here. Who died?"

"Good question." He ignored her sarcasm and sat at the other end of the table. "I thought maybe you could answer some questions for me about the death of Rosie Adams. No bullshit. Just tell me what happened. How do you know Pearce Jones?" He looked straight into those big green saucer-sized eyes and was drawn in like he was hypnotized. He had to quickly look away. *Snap out of it! You've seen this kind before.* He could smell her Chanel No. 5 perfume. Her lips were shiny and red. She looked at him like she wanted to kiss him. She smiled. The little diamond in her front tooth snapped him out of it.

She began twisting her hair with her right hand. "What makes you think I know anything?" She had cleavage popping right out at him. *How do they let these people in here like this? There ought to be a law against being so sexy.* Her skin was flawless. He went outside in the lobby for a moment then walked outside to get some fresh evening air. He took a few deep breaths and returned to her. This time she sat with her legs crossed. He was ready now to fight back against all this womanism going on. "Okay, Miss Rogers, I'm going to start reading you your rights if you don't start talking now." He hesitated and looked at her. She was quiet with her arms folded looking down.

He spoke. "Anything you say can and will be held against you. You have the right—"

She cut him off. "Okay, I'll tell you about my involvement with Pearce. I know what happened to the money from the robbery in 1971. Tom Adams stole it from me in Valdosta and Pearce was acting like he didn't care about me anymore. I was mad at Tom and Pearce. They both did me wrong and all they cared about was seeing Angela and her mother who was in the hospital."

Sergeant Eddie spoke softly. "What happened to Mrs. Adams?"

"I was going to do in Ms. Rosie to get even but I changed my mind like I do a lot. Sometimes I like Pearce and sometimes I don't. And yes, I wanted to make them all mad. I just played around with the plug a little and I plugged it back in and left. She was fine when I left."

"Wait a minute. You're telling me that Tom, Angela's father, stole the money from you that was taken in the robbery and you left the plug intact in Mrs. Adams' room? Why should I believe you?"

"Ask that no-good Pearce. He was there at the hospital and he saw me leave. Maybe his ass did it. He said he never liked the old lady anyway. I didn't think she was all that special and neither is her trifling daughter, Angela. She had Pearce thinking she was queen bee and all the time she was having an affair with that white attorney. But Pearce acts like he can't live without her. He's gonna learn. Messing around with her type. She'll get any man in trouble. Look what happened to him from following her out here. Her and her mom."

"Oh," said Sergeant Eddie, "I can see how you are much better for him than Angela is. You help him hold some money from a robbery and play around with the vent plug on his mother-in-law's oxygen machine. Okay, Ms. Rogers or Ms. Bitch as you are better known, I can hold you in a cell or you can stay in town. Something tells me you're not going to go far from Pearce and something tells me Pearce is not going too far from Angela. I suggest you wait in the lobby for your man. He's processing out now."

She gave him a shocked look and a smile. "What?"

He put on his black wool scarf and buttoned up his trench coat. "Yep, just for you. I'm letting him go because I think you two are good for each other. And another thing. You seem like a really nice person."

"Hey, I'm really sorry about Mrs. Adams. You do believe me, don't you?"

He glanced at his gold Bulova watch. "Sure. Pretty much everything you told me. Are you in love with Pearce?"

"I was back in the day and we spent some wonderful time in Chicago. Maybe I was kinda taken with his beautiful smile and the way his tongue touched my lips." She licked her lips while looking at him. She sighed and looked at him with those big saucer eyes.

He turned around and headed toward the front door then turned back around as if he forgot something. He was bold enough to look right into those dark green eyes. "Hey, check out the beach sometimes. It's gorgeous at night."

Sergeant Eddie knew he took a small risk letting Pearce go so fast but the statute of limitations on the robbery was about up for the bank robbery. The decision to release or hold him for trial would be the Superior Court judge's. Sergeant Eddie made sure he had let Pearce know that he could pick him up in a heartbeat and drag him right back into jail if he caused anybody any trouble.

Later that night he set his brandy glass down, put another log in the fireplace and poked the red-hot embers on the burning hickory log. Lulu sat on the white bearskin rug doing her nightly sit-ups with her knees bent. She counted, "One, two, three."

"Will you stop it already!" Eddie said. "I'm trying to figure out a friggin' case here and you ain't helping none with all that damn counting." He mocked her, "One, two three, four. Can't you find something else to do besides exercise?" She stopped, looked at him and put her head down.

Sergeant Eddie calmed down and said in a soothing tone, "You look good now, baby, even better than you did eight years ago when I first saw you."

"Ah Eddie, sometimes you can be so sweet. Come here. Momma loves you. I'll help you figure it out. Tell me what's new."

He joined her on the floor where they sat with their backs resting against the love seat. "I got Pearce and that so-called Ms. Bitch, Connie, being tailed. Now I'm trying to locate Tom without upsetting Angela any more. He picked a very convenient time to come back to L.A. Something is not coming to the surface on this one and I just can't get a handle on it. I know it wasn't Pearce or Connie. Don't even think it was the doctor because he told me about the note he wrote to Angela. I haven't ruled out Angela yet, nor her daddy that came up out of the blue. Her auntie is still in the running and so is Carl."

"Honey, didn't you say Ms. B. wiped off the plug? Just played around with it. Well I can see how you ruled her out because if she did it she would not say she was even there. Why are you ruling out Pearce? After all, he has a long record. For goodness' sake, Eddie, he committed a robbery and he ran away from justice, lied to his wife a few times, took the baby and left her at the train station and came to the hospital without anybody even knowing he was coming. Not even Angela. The so-called love of his life."

Eddie lay on the white rug in front of the warm fire and let her massage his shoulders. "I know Pearce didn't do it even though most of the pieces fit and I'm sure he had mixed feelings for his mother-in-law. There's good and bad in everybody. He may be a criminal, and not the smartest one, mind you. I wouldn't under-estimate him either. He's definitely got a lot of potential and could do some damage if he wanted to."

"Honey. I trust you know what you're doing, but let me tell you what I read in my latest edition of the *Inside Scope* detective magazine. They say the person that's least expected is sometimes the one to watch and the apparently guilty might be innocent." She rubbed his head and hugged him. "I love you honey, and you know what you're doing."

He answered, "Yeah, babe. Someone with Pearce's qualities for sure."

"Why do you keep suspecting Angela? I think she loved her mom too much and plus was an only child. Only children can't carry that burden of guilt. They are just too darn nice, Eddie. I know 'cause I'm an only child and I could not do that but I could get my point across to someone else to make them do it. Carl obviously worships the ground Angela walks on. And he's an attorney. He might think he's above the law."

"He may think that way and a lot of attorneys think they are above the law. Anyone could think they are above the law if they want to commit a crime. That way they feel guilt free. Attorneys are human too but Carl doesn't fit the profile, plus if he did it that would make them both guilty of murder in the first degree."

"Eddie," she said sleepily, "that could explain why they're making wedding plans. So they can't testify against each other if called to."

Eddie answered, "Maybe, maybe, maybe. Let's keep 'em on the back burner for now. They don't grab me yet either. He's got reason to do it and I could be wrong, but I don't think he has guts to do it. It's gotta be someone with courage beyond measurement."

Lulu asked, "Could it be someone they all know? Who would they know with all that courage?"

"Maybe it's someone they don't know who knows them."

"Wow, Eddie. Who's missing from their lives?"

"Someone with courage."

Chapter 18

MAZIE MET TOM AT SAMANTHA'S TEA CUP on the corner of Crenshaw and Washington around the corner from her apartment. The aroma of fresh-baked blueberry muffins filled the air.

Tom set the menu down and asked, "Mazie, tell me what you know about Joe and Rosie's boys."

"Tom, I didn't want to tell Angela this, but Rosie had been seeing one of those boys. I know she been seeing him 'cause one of the nurses told me who came and went. Some young man came to see her and his name is Joseph Jr. Looks a lot like Angela. In his late twenties or early thirties. Nobody knew where he came from but Rosie must have known him. He stayed quite a while sometimes. We need to find this young man who came to see Rosie but where in the world would we start looking?"

"I don't know, Mazie," said Tom. "You think that might have been him? One of the twins? Where is the other one then? I think Rosie would have told me by now if she knew where those boys were. Don't you think she would have found me somehow and told me that? But then, she was known for keeping things from me. Especially the fact that she had an affair and those boys were not mine in the first place. I have a feeling about things like this and I bet you we're closer than we think." The waiter came and offered them some more steaming hot coffee, asking, "How are you folks doing? Need anything else?"

"No, I'm good, sweetie. Tom, you want anything else?"

Tom shook his head and waved the waiter away.

Mazie looked at her reflection in her compact mirror while she powdered her shiny nose. Then she quickly looked for her red lipstick in her little lizard purse. Her heart-shaped mouth looked just like Rose's. "Since we can't solve this thing right now I guess I better go on home."

The slender waiter put his well-manicured hand on the table between them and said, "You two seem like you want something else." He removed his hand and walked swiftly to the back of the restaurant. Mazie picked up a blue business card with silver and red stars on it.

Tom sighed. "What's that card say? What's he selling? Everybody got a hustle."

"Psychic reading. Just one dollar a minute. Guaranteed results. Find loved ones, old friends, missing money, jewelry. Find your lucky numbers. Money back if you are not satisfied with the results. Twenty-four hours. Call me now."

Tom yawned, and put a two-dollar tip on the table. "Whose card is it? What's the name of the company and who is this fabulous con artist who knows so darn much?"

"Well," Mazie said, "this all-knowing wonderful company is called Pusha's Private Line." She looked at him, smiling. "It gets better. 'Credit cards accepted. Call me now or be forever in the dark.'"

Tom sighed. "How can we all call her now? She can't talk to everybody at one time. That is if she is so good at what she does. Somebody else must be taking some calls. And you sure not going to talk to no lady named Pusha. Hey, I know that game and game it is. You still lookin' at that card?" He shook his head. "Mazie, you want to find those boys, don't you? Here's my credit card. Go to the phone and throw away some money. Who knows? She might make a lucky guess." He laughed. "Pusha Private Line!"

Mazie dialed the pay phone on the wall and sat down on the partly cushioned stool. While it rang she read the graffiti on the nearby wall. The phone rang and rang then someone answered and she heard, "Give me that phone. It's my turn to say Pusha Private Line!"

"No it's not. It's my turn!" Then she heard yelling. "Aunt Pusha! Bobbie won't let me say Pusha Private Line and she know it's my turn!" Then Mazie heard crying and "I'm telling Mama on you!"

Mazie started to hang up the phone then but she kept seeing her sister Rose's face and she could hear her saying, "Don't give up looking for my children."

Mazie sighed and waited. Then what sounded like a ten-year-old girl said, "Pusha Private Line. Guaranteed results. May I help you?" She was chewing and popping her gum.

Mazie spoke softly as if trying not to break a spell. "Can I speak to Pusha?"

"Who dis?" the gum chewer continued.

"My name is Mazie. I got her card and need some..."

Before she could finish, the gum chewer yelled out to someone in the background.

"Aunt Pusha! Somebody want you!"

Mazie heard the sound of someone in the background, then the little girl spoke into the phone again in her normal gum-popping voice. "You got a card with money on it? What the numbers on the card?"

Mazie read the numbers off the credit card to this child who repeated them back to her. Mazie knew this was crazy but she had to try everything to find those boys that belonged to her late sister. And Rosie would want her to. Poor Rosie.

Then a raspy sounding voice came on the line in a whisper. "Pusha speaking. All wise and all knowing. Mazie, you need my help? What you want? Satisfaction guaranteeeeed!"

Mazie looked at Tom who was reading the sports section in the *Daily Record* and occasionally glancing at his sister-in-law. He could not read her expression and had no clue if it was good news or not so he went on checking the high school basketball stats. Crenshaw High Varsity was in the lead in the boys' division.

Mazie looked surprised as she hung up the phone. She walked quickly back to the table where Tom was. "Pusha said the boys would be at Venice Beach at six in the evening tomorrow. Sunday. Even though it will be somewhat crowded there she said we'll find them. She asked me some questions about their parents."

"Yeah," Tom said, "that's how they reel you in. Tell 'em all your business!"

Mazie stood patiently while he finished with the skepticism. He looked at her and sighed, "Okay, give tell me the rest of it and I'll try to keep an open mind."

Mazie perked up again. "She said since both their parents had played basketball and other sports, there was a good chance they would be at the Sunday evening tournament. And Tom, you know everybody does go there either to watch or play."

"Yeah, yeah, I know."

"She said they would be on the courts by the cotton candy and popcorn machine wearing blue shorts and white jerseys. And I will know them because they look just like Angela but they have reddish brown hair."

"You believe that woman?" Tom said. "Never mind. Never mind. I'll pick you up but maybe we won't tell Angela somebody named Pusha is helping us find her brothers unless we find them."

Chapter 19

SERGEANT EDDIE AND LULU FINISHED JOGGING in the sunset at Venice Beach around five thirty and sat on the bleachers waiting for the six o'clock championship basketball games. The two County league teams, one from Baldwin Hills and the other from Los Angeles, had made it to the finals and the winners would get a two thousand dollar prize.

Mazie and Tom watched the game and these two boys were very good, but Baldwin Hills beat their team by five points. Tom stood up. "Let's go and talk to them. They do look like my Rosie. Dear God, what is going on?"

Tom approached them after a few minutes of watching them congratulate the other team members and gathering their stuff. "Hey, good game, you guys. Sorry you guys lost. My bet was on you all. Baldwin Hills is getting better over the years though. I know Los Angeles got the better players but everybody gotta lose sometime and that was just a lot of luck. If they win again next year then we'll say they can play. Hey, what are your names?"

One of the boys looked at the other one and then back at Tom. "I'm Joseph and he's John. We're just fine. What do you want?"

John interrupted, "Hey man, don't pay any attention to him. He's a sore loser and he thinks because he is my twin he can play ball as good as me but he's mistaken."

Joseph spoke again. "Hey, let's get to the bottom line. We know who you are, Tom. You are our real mother's husband who left her and our sister, Angela."

He looked at Mazie and extended his hand to her and she held onto it. "You are our aunt Mazie. Our mom told us about you and showed us your pictures."

"Oh my God," she answered. "I can't believe this is all happening." She hugged them both while Tom looked on. Then the boys hugged him too.

John said, "We saw all of you at the hospital too but we didn't want to say anything to anybody 'cause momma Rosie said you couldn't deal with us seeing as how she cheated on you. She said she was going to straighten everything out one day when she got out of the hospital because our sister was coming back in town and we were just waiting for our mom to get better."

"My God," Mazie said, "we can't believe that lady Pusha was right. Where you all been staying all this time? And how is Joseph, your father? It's so good to see you two boys at last. Come on over to my house and meet Angela. Come with me and Tom. Don't you think they should come on over, Tom?" They were all sitting on the wooden bench now and the orange sun sank deeper and deeper into the Pacific as the crowd of onlookers thinned out.

Just then, Sergeant Eddie got up from the damp grass under the low palm trees he had moved to after Lulu went home. He folded his newspaper neatly and threw it with extra strength into the nearby trashcan. "Damn," he thought, "Pusha was right again. She led me right to these two boys and all I did was tell her about the Converse shoe prints found near Mrs. Adams' hospital bed." He had done Pusha a big favor by helping her sister get released from the forgery charges so she could take care of her own five children. Pusha had called him when she found out about all the matching Converse shoe prints at the bedside. It was apparent to Sergeant Eddie that there were possibly twin boys involved because of all the prints at the same time and it was just too many to belong to one person.

She called him to offer him a deal because she was supposed to be a psychic. He figured she knew a lot about that Crenshaw section of Los Angeles and some of everybody's business. And true to her word, she told him somebody named Mazie was also looking for them boys.

Pusha also told him that she told Mazie where to look. Pusha added that she felt the boys might be in some kinda trouble anyway and that she might be protecting them. Sergeant Eddie summed it all up real good. Pusha was tired of taking care of all five of her sister's children so she didn't feel bad about betraying Mazie. "Well," he thought, "a deal is a deal."

He witnessed this tear-jerking reunion and now he had to come forward and grab the two suspects. He had called headquarters for a backup and waited for the black-and-white to pull up to the curve. He looked at Tom first as he approached the four of them. "How are we doing on this lovely evening? I'm Sergeant Best from LAPD." He looked at the young men. "I need the two of you to come with me downtown. I have some questions about the death of Mrs. Rosie Adams. And I do believe she was your mother." He put the handcuffs on them while two other officers stood by. Tom put his arm around Mazie's shoulder.

"What's this about? I'm sure these are good boys. Officer, there's gotta be some kind of mistake here."

Sergeant Eddie answered, "This is routine questioning for now. When we get some answers you all will be the first to know."

Tom and Mazie stood silently watching the boys being taken away while their rights were read to them. John looked back at them. "You should have been a man, Tom. Then our momma would not have messed up. Think about that!"

Mazie yelled, "We'll be here to help you."

"Yeah," Tom yelled, "just be quiet. Don't say nothing. We'll help you out."

He and Mazie looked at each other and said to each other at the same time, "Carl Finch."

After the boys were secure in the back of the car, Sergeant Eddie came back to the grass and said to Tom, "These boys are going to need a lot of help."

He answered, "I can see that. You better know what you are doing. Them boys ain't got nothing to do with nothing!"

"Oh yeah, you want to come down to the station yourself? Showing up after all these years. Perfect timing. Wouldn't you say? Especially right after you just took out the insurance policy on your wife. I bet you were going to share that money with Angela, huh?"

Tom started to answer and Sergeant Eddie stopped him. "I was pretty much sold on you being the killer, but then I had you checked out and realized you were not even in town when all this happened. Good thing I checked you out, huh? People take out policies all the time, especially on estranged spouses."

But Tom answered anyway. "If you did your homework you would know that we took out policies on each other because we were getting up in age and plus she had not been feeling too well. We thought at least the boys and Angela would be taken care of if something happened to one of us."

"Good deal. See you all later. Stay close. Families need to stay close." Then he got in the black-and-white squad car and drove away.

Chapter 20

TOM SAID, "THIS IS ALL TOO MUCH TO TELL ANGELA ABOUT. The going to jail and even the fact that we found those boys."

Mazie said, "We gonna have to tell her anyway. No time would ever be ideal for this, so we tell her as soon as we see her."

They drove the Cadillac to the apartment where Angela and Carl were. Tom said, "When we go in take a deep breath and start talking."

Sergeant Eddie questioned John and then Joseph Jr. separately to see if their stories matched. "Okay, John, we know you and your brother were at the hospital visiting Mrs. Adams. I want straight answers." He looked him in the eyes. "Do you know

Mrs. Adams was your mother? Did you or your brother unplug the machine at her bedside?"

John answered slowly looking the sergeant in the eyes. "I don't know nothing and my brother don't know nothing either. We love her and we know she loved us. You are wasting your time talking to me and I want to go home now."

"You can go pretty soon. Just relax. Going to see how your brother is doing. If he is thirsty or anything." With that he left the room and walked down the narrow hallway to the other interrogation room where Joseph was sitting. He was writing on a yellow legal pad with a number two pencil very rapidly. He looked up at Sergeant Eddie and back down at this paper and kept writing as fast as he could.

Eddie sat down across the table and lit a cigarette. Cursing himself for breaking his vow to quit smoking, but he needed one now.

"Ah, writing your memoirs? I suppose you are going to give that to me to mail. Need an envelope?"

Joseph put the pencil down and looked up and said slowly, "This is for my brother John. Letting him know what to do. 'Cause he will be all alone now except for our dad who is in poor health now. Me and John never been separated before but now maybe he can finally be with our sister, Angela, if she don't think she too good for the likes of us illegitimates."

Sergeant Eddie knew better than to rush things like this. Joseph might be on the verge of confessing or he might be playing a game. "Do you want me to read that?"

"No need to read. I did it. I unplugged Mom's machine because she asked me to but I didn't want to get into any trouble so I hurried up and got out of there. She was so pitiful and so weak-looking. She kept saying her stomach hurt and her head hurt and those big brown eyes were pleading with me. It just wasn't right for her to be like that. Couldn't let her suffer. My brother don't know about it yet but I'm telling him in this letter to go on and don't worry about me. That's all I can say. Is there anything else you want to know, Sergeant?"

Sergeant Eddie got up and stood in front of the window and looked out at the hustle and bustle on the boulevard for a moment. His heart became heavy as he thought to himself, "Her own child." He turned around and looked at Joseph again. The kid was still writing.

"Joseph, no need to say anything more. Your sister's fiancé is an attorney and they are on the way. Until then, keep writing." He shut the door softly and sat on the cushioned leather bench in the deserted hallway. Tears rolled down his face. A voice inside him kept saying, *Her own child. Her own child. Oh my God, he's just a baby.* He wept for Mrs. Adams and for the twins who were now in deep trouble. He wept for all the people who had to suffer and wanted a way out. And most of all for his own mother who he needed to go and visit. He remembered Lulu who kept saying, "You need to go see your mother. She's getting old. You only got one, Eddie."

He went to the pay phone on the wall and called his mom just to say he loved her and he and Lulu would drive up the coast to see her soon.

* * *

Once Carl and Angela got all the news that the boys were found and were taken to jail for questioning, they went downtown early the next morning leaving Mazie and Tom with Candi.

They made their way through the congested rush hour traffic. Angela drove the Mercedes while Carl sat next to her looking through his files and making some notes. She squeezed his left arm with her right hand. "Honey, what are we going to do for them?"

Carl took his glasses off and stuck them in his shirt pocket. "First of all, sweetheart, you are not handling this case. This is my case, sweetheart, because you are not an attorney and you are too close to them even though you have been apart from them practically your whole life. They are identical twins and identical twins stick together even if they both have to go down for a crime. One will risk his freedom to keep the other one free. One of them could be lying but they both have to tell me the truth or it's no deal, Angela. That is, by far, the best way you can help them. Tell the boys that under no circumstances are they to lie to me. We don't know if they have been charged or what the charges might be. Let's just get downtown and see what happens."

"Oh my, Carl. This is all a nightmare. And the truth is maybe they did what everybody else wanted to do or at least a few people. They must have some kinda evidence to hold them. And it didn't help for Joseph to confess. Now they have to hold both of them."

Angela and Carl made it to the jail area and Angela didn't know how to feel when she saw the boys. Sergeant Eddie had arranged for her to see them with a couple of deputies present.

The boys explained to her why they had stayed away, not knowing if she would be glad to see them or not. Their mother had told them she would explain everything to everybody when Angela got back to Los Angeles but then Rose got sick.

Angela did her best to stay calm. "My fiancé is going to help the two of you even though one of you confessed." She turned to John. "The police think you both are guilty and one of you will help the other one to stay free. I don't want to know what happened now, but you have to tell Mr. Finch, my fiancé, who is representing you all, the whole truth and nothing but the fucking truth." She continued looking at them with a stern face. Then she started crying. "Are you or are you not going to tell the truth?" They answered her together. "Yes we are."

"I can't be in the room with you and Carl but he's good. He knows what he is doing and he will take good care of you two."

She was allowed to hug them before she left and then Carl came into the room.

"How are you two doing this morning? I know this is hard to do deal with. First, I want to make sure you know what they are trying to charge you all with and what your options are. They have some Converse shoe prints that are very similar, but there is a slight difference in one of the pairs. I guess there was a tiny rock stuck in one of the soles. And there were more prints from that shoe."

Carl looked down at their Converse shoes and paused. Then he snapped open his briefcase and sat down across the table from them with a yellow legal pad. "Okay, why don't you guys start telling me what you do for a living. Go to school, work?"

"We go to the college of performing arts in Los Angeles. This is our second year," said John.

Joseph volunteered, "We take urban drama."

Carl continued, "Actors? Great profession. Urban drama? Who would have thought? Now I need you two to be completely honest with me. Did either of you pull that plug out? Remember now, I'm on your side."

The boys looked at each other, then at Carl. Then they said together, "I did it."

Carl slammed his fist on the beat-up wooden table. "Damn it! I said tell me who did it. Or did both of you do it? Okay, if that's what you two want, both of you are going to burn. I might as well plead you two guilty now. Right?"

Sergeant Eddie was about to knock on the door to see how Carl and the boys were doing when a female deputy with tight-fitting khakis stopped him in the hallway. She smiled. "We got that report ready. You wanna come take a look?"

Sergeant Eddie paused a minute then knocked on the door anyway. It quickly opened and he leaned in. "Hold that thought, counselor." He left the room and everybody waited silently, not hardly moving. Sergeant Eddie came back in a flash and called Carl outside the door. "Never mind, counselor. It looks like the hospital installed an experimental surveillance camera in that unit some time ago but unfortunately it only recorded a few minutes every hour."

Carl said, "Interesting."

"The concern was possible interference with all the other electrical equipment on the Intensive Care Unit."

"Okay, what's the deal, Sergeant? I suppose someone was picked up on it?"

"Yes," Sergeant Eddie answered. "It is fortunate for us and unfortunate for one of your clients. And believe me this was no acting job." He opened the door, poked his head in and spoke. "John, come on. You are free to go. Just walk right on out."

John looked around at his brother and said, "Don't worry, you'll be out soon. They don't know what they're doing." Then he went on out the opened door.

Sergeant Eddie continued, "Joseph, it's been a long day. Whatever else you have to say you can say to your defense attorney here. See you all later!"

The next day Carl looked at the film from the camera and sure enough it was Joseph pulling out the plug. The camera could not be lying. Would the DA be willing to plea bargain with a mercy killing of a mother by a son? A son who was gone so long and didn't want to see her suffer? Or would they think that was a reason for him to kill her? She had left them with their father who was good for nothing. Could Joseph have hated her?

Carl didn't want to think of answers that would make him sick. A child doing away with his parent was hard to imagine even if the picture was right there in living color. He would have to come up with a good defense and he wondered now if there *was* a defense. He tossed all the ideas in his head. Insanity? Revenge? Anger? Compassion was the only defense. What would the DA call it? What motive would they come up with? It didn't matter. The proof was in the pudding. There was a guilty child, and his brother didn't even know anything about it according to the letter

Joseph wrote to him. That was why the DA let John go. According to all the records there was no history of mental illness or criminal background. What would make him cross that line? Even he said he did it because he wanted to help her.

But California law stated that mercy killing is a crime. Carl knew that California had several laws pending on the books about mercy killing when he had passed the bar exam some years ago. Nonetheless right now any act of compassion killing was still punishable by life in the pen. Carl thought about his own father, McKenzie Finch, who stole the deed from the poor old black woman who had worked for his grandfather, Old Man Finch. And just what would my ornery old grandfather do in a case like this?

Carl knew he would have to appeal to the state's moral judgment and sympathy. This was a case of that little area between the lines of the scripted law and humanity. Which one would prevail? Whatever the outcome, he knew it was going to either push the law forward or drag it backwards.

Excerpt

Here's an excerpt from Abrendal Austin's next novel featuring Angela Jones. Log on to www.blackpennypress.com for details and publication date.

IN VALDOSTA, GEORGIA, MIKE SAT BY THE BANK in his lawn chair watching the small sailing boats and large fishing vessels floating on the Swanee River. He enjoyed watching the bluebirds and red robins flying around and chirping. He could smell the damp earth and the scent from all the creatures in the dark river. This area was always quiet during the day and he knew he only had an hour here until he got back to his accounting duties inside the busy inn.

He had his mind on his upcoming trip to New York City. He could see the bright lights in Times Square and he welcomed another trip on the ferry to Ellis Island to see the Statue of Liberty.

He always got a rush standing there at the very top in the torch. He felt like a king up there. No wife to bug him. No silly-ass friends. Yes, up there he was ahead of the game and the hustlers on the busy crowded streets below. The last time he was there he felt like a king on his throne. "Look at me, peons. Mere mortals. I'm the boss of New York City. Bring me all the fancy food and wine and everybody do what the hell I say. Ha, ha."

Someone shook him. "Mike, Mike. Wake up, man. Wake up!"

"Oh no," thought Mike. It was Jamie. One of the last people he wanted to see. The other one was Stella, who took his part of the money that Angela's father gave them to take her that enve- lope. She never gave it back. Now Jamie stood here messing up his nice dream of New York. He hadn't even told them to bring him all the pretty women yet. He sat up and looked at Jamie.

"What in the hell are you doing here? I told you I was through with you and Stella."

"Look, man," Jamie said, "I'm trying to tell you Stella got your two hundred dollars for you. Man, she gave me three hundred because she took so long giving it to me. Said she had to do something with the money but she's going to give you an extra hundred too. If you don't want it, man, I'll go on back to cutting the weeds in the rose garden."

Mike stood up now. "Where she at? I sure need my money for my trip to the Big Apple this year. Damn! I wish she would have given it to you."

Stella came out of the rose garden with a big smile and some tight little yellow shorts on that looked like she was poured in. A matching halter top lifted her 38-C cups way up high and it was buttoned so tight that the buttons looked like they were going to pop any minute. She had a dark tan and her long shiny legs were muscular and slender. Her long red hair was now a dark brown pixie cut. To Mike, she looked so different but still gorgeous. He wondered if her attitude would be any different.

"Hi, guys," she said. She sat down on the wooden bench and crossed her legs with her red satin pumps sparkling.

Mike looked at her and she looked so innocent. He tried to be serious but it was hard. Finally he found his voice. "Where is my money, Stella? I don't want any games today."

She answered, "I got your money. I went to Atlantic City, New Jersey with you all's money and won a nice little jackpot. Now, I want to share it with you two."

Mike said, "Just give me the two hundred you owe me and I'll be cool. Don't come with no funny style stories. I gotta go back to work soon."

Stella smiled. "I won some nice money to share with you all but first we could at least have some tea. Oh, this time my darling mother sent us some cranberry cream pastries along with her special lemon tea all the way from Germany. You all can take some home to your wives, too."

Mike gave up. "Okay, damn it! How much did you win?"

"Fifteen thousand dollars. I'm going to give you each five thousand for your vacation this year or to spend any way you want. Isn't that nice of me? Don't you forgive me now for taking so long to pay you all back the money from that guy who said he was Angela's father?"

"That's a lot of money and I'll feel better if you just go ahead and pay me mine now. Then I'll have all the tea you want," said Mike.

She said, "Come on, sit down while I separate it."

Jamie started putting the cups on the tree stump that doubled as their table. Stella held two large bundles of money in her hands. Then a guy and a tall red-headed female with saucer-sized green eyes and long slender legs walked up behind them and faced Stella. Mike and Jamie turned around when they heard their footsteps and saw the surprised look on Stella's face. The guy stood there with a big silly grin. Mike took in a deep breath and let it out slowly.

"What the hell are you two doing here, Pearce?"

www.abrendalaustin.com